Ghostly Music

Later, Tim went to see Beth. Lying in semi-darkness, she winced when he opened the door, letting in the light. "Do you want to talk about it?" he asked, but she didn't answer. He sat on the bed. "Beth, we've always shared things."

"Go away, Tim," she whispered. "My head hurts too much."

"Please, Beth."

She seemed touched at last by his concern. Struggling to sit up, she said, "I saw her again. The ghost. She was outside. She began to clap. It was horrible." She stared at Tim in despair. "Why me?" she whispered. "Why is she picking on me?"

HIPPO GHOST

Ghostly Music

Richard Brown

Hippo

Scholastic Children's Books
Commonwealth House, 1–19 New Oxford Street,
London WC1A 1NU, UK
a division of Scholastic Ltd
London ~ New York ~ Toronto ~ Sydney ~ Auckland

First published by Scholastic Ltd, 1997

Text copyright © Richard Brown, 1997

ISBN 0 590 19174 8

All rights reserved
Typeset by TW Typesetting, Midsomer Norton, Avon
Printed by Cox & Wyman Ltd, Reading, Berks.

10 9 8 7 6 5 4 3 2 1

TO PAMELA
in whose house this ghost materialized!

AUGUST 31st 1912

Helen thought her father might be out for the whole morning. He had said as much at the breakfast table but had been uncharacteristically vague about it. She waited impatiently in her room, combing her long red hair, until she heard the heavy front door bang and the car start up and chug away. A cloud seemed to lift from the house.

In her long white dress she hurried down the broad staircase and into the shadowy hall. Pale sunlight slanting through the coloured glass window on the landing cast a pool of warmth, and for a moment Helen stood in it, catching her breath. She listened for movements in the house. Miss Marshall, the governess, had just gone out on an errand. She could hear the housekeeper talking in low tones with the cook in the kitchen. Upstairs, her mother lay silent, brought down by influenza. Helen had the morning to herself. That was so rare she felt tense with anticipation.

Half an hour a day – that was all the doctor and her father would allow. Half an hour with her beloved piano: a starvation diet.

Once inside the music-room, she had to lie briefly on the chaise-longue to gather her scant energies and calm herself. Fatigue was always present now. The hollow, gnawing pain in her chest seemed more insistent than ever.

On the chaise-longue was her manuscript book – thick, brown, embossed, with creamy pages – in which she wrote her secret compositions for piano. Her mother had praised her for her application to this – but in the same way that she had praised her for the neat stitching in her sampler; she saw no essential difference between the two. Her father, she knew, thought her scribblings were childish and gave them no thought. But she did not mind; it left her free to write what she wanted.

Lately, she had been in a fever of creativity. One extraordinary night, the shape of a whole sonata had come into her mind. It had played in her head like spectral music, in maddening, tantalizing snatches. The strain of working it out on the piano and scoring it in her manuscript book had sapped her energy in a way which had alarmed her. But she drove herself on, obscurely aware that time was running out. Now the second movement, which she had begun a few days before, was proving unexpectedly difficult.

Beating back the fatigue and pain, she sat at the piano and opened her manuscript book. She picked up her favourite pen, found it was empty, and filled it with black ink. Then she was ready. She closed her eyes and listened intently to the music in her head. She tried it out on the piano and wrote it down when she knew she had got it right.

Half an hour went by in the space of what seemed like five minutes. The house remained silent. She pressed on. Her temperature rose. Her body grew sticky. The pain in her chest seemed to spread. Every symptom told her to stop. But she was in the grip of the music.

The grandfather clock in the hall struck eleven-thirty. She was nearly halfway through the second movement when she heard her father's car chug back into the gravel drive. She froze. It could have been John, the chauffeur, returning. Instinctively, however, she knew it was her father. The vague fear she had always felt for him welled up; she knew the housekeeper would tell him she had been playing the piano all *morning. She heard the front door open, voices in the hall. Heavy footsteps approached the music-room.*

As her father opened the door, a sharp pain, of a fierceness she had never felt before, shot through her chest, into her throat, as if something was bursting. The nib of her pen snapped and ink blotted her manuscript. It spread slowly, like blood. Far away, she heard her father shouting, the rasp of his words coinciding with each new spasm of pain. Then she felt herself being lifted, rising into darkness, a darkness like velvet closing over her mind.

Chapter 1
The Invitation

Beth was dazzled by the fierce sunlight cutting through the leaves. Pausing by an ash tree, she closed her eyes and listened to the hollow, random notes in the warm air: a pheasant calling, a pigeon flapping noisily from a treetop, a bluebottle buzzing. In between, there were moments of silence, as if the wood was holding its breath. Beth always came here when she needed to think.

Not far away a stick snapped. She scanned the trees in faint alarm. The last thing she wanted was to meet someone she knew. Not now. Not this morning when things were so tense, exciting, different. There was a long silence. Just as she was about to move off, she heard a faint cough. Was there someone there? Watching her? Nervously, she moved on, making her way up an overgrown path through tall, shadowy trees.

She had come down to breakfast that morning to find Tim, her elder brother, leaning over the table staring at something in the local paper. He pointed to a photograph.

"They've recognized your genius at last," he said mockingly. "Look." She peered over his shoulder. "It says here you're a young prodigy."

"A what?" She narrowed her eyes suspiciously.

In the photograph, Beth was standing by a piano on the school stage. The picture had been taken at the school concert a few days ago, after a recital she had given to a hall packed with parents and pupils. She looked tall, thin, flushed, her red hair flowing over her shoulders. Recalling the loud applause, the shouts of encore, she flushed again. It was embarrassing to see it all there, her feelings of relief and pride, of a deep wish come true, summed up in a bright picture and a bland caption. "What's a prodigy, then?" she asked, feigning indifference.

"It's a sort of superbrat," Tim said with a grin, delighted at her discomfort. She turned her back on him; but he could see she was fascinated by the idea. "So now I've got to live with a prodigy. To bask in reflected glory," he teased. "They'll point to me in the street and say, 'See him? He's the brother of that amazing prodigy, you know, the one...'"

"Oh, shut up," said Beth. But Tim couldn't stop talking about it all through breakfast.

She thought, I must get away and think it all through.

She heard another stick snap underfoot, nearer this time. She paused again, trying to find out what was making the noise. Then, moving on, she turned a corner in the path. She was brought up sharply by a dark figure moving down the path towards her. The light turned the tall figure into a silhouette, a moving shadow. Beth's instinct was to run.

The figure was of a tall and fairly elderly woman. Beth stood to one side to let her pass, but the woman stopped a few feet away from her. Beth glanced apprehensively at her. Despite the heat, the woman wore a long, dark-grey, old-fashioned coat. On her feet was a stout pair of lace-up boots. She was carrying a battered-looking shopping bag over her arm. She stared at the girl keenly. Beth's scalp crept; she hated being stared at. She felt unable to move. The woman examined her closely. Beth felt the woman's gaze penetrate to the very beating of her heart.

Beth managed to say good morning. The woman smiled. "Good morning, my dear," she said in a firm, deep voice. To the girl's surprise, she held out her hand and said, "I believe you are Beth Brooke. Am I right?"

Shifting slightly to avoid the sun's glare, Beth looked into the woman's face, at the strong features and intent grey eyes. She realized, then, that she knew the woman. Gran had spoken about her once or twice. Miss Murdoch – that was it. Oh, and wasn't she…? Beth looked at her more closely, her heart suddenly beating faster. Hadn't she once been a concert pianist – surely Gran had said that – or was she just imagining it?

"Hello," she said uncertainly, taking Miss Murdoch's hand and giving it a quick shake.

The woman said, "We've not really met before, I know, but I'm sure you've noticed me about. I've been meaning to talk to you for some time."

Miss Murdoch shifted her gaze to her shopping bag, moving it from one arm to another while she thought how to proceed. She said, "When I saw your picture in the local paper today, I said to myself, 'Yes, she's the one. It's time this girl and I met.'" She stopped and, leaning forward a little, she added more quietly, "It's time you and I worked together. What do you think?"

There was something about the way Miss Murdoch said those last few words that made Beth feel uneasy. She edged back and took a swift look up and down the path. It was empty. They were all alone. The wood was uncannily still.

Miss Murdoch smiled again. "But I'm alarming you, child," she said. "I'm sorry, I don't mean to. You see, when I read in the paper how well you played in the school concert, I was so pleased – and not just for you, for myself too." Beth stared at her, baffled. "Let me explain," the woman said. She lifted a strand of grey hair from her face and thought for a moment. "Ever since I was about your age, I cared for nothing but the piano. For years I was a concert pianist, playing all over the world." She paused. "But because of this –" and she held out hands that showed signs of arthritis – "I have been unable to play much lately. I can still play for myself, of course; but now I only take in pupils. Promising ones, you understand." She waited for Beth to respond.

Beth tried to think of something polite to say. "Were you famous?" she asked, not sure if this was the right thing to say.

"Oh, I don't know about famous," Miss Murdoch laughed, shaking her head. "But I've always enjoyed teaching, especially those with real talent."

10

Beth thought she understood now. She put her hands into her jean pockets and half-looked at the woman, wondering if she had guessed correctly.

"Who is teaching you at the moment?" Miss Murdoch suddenly asked.

Beth frowned. This was something of a sore point. "I'm having some lessons at school, with Mrs Fletcher; but she only comes once a week. I did once have a private tutor before Dad went abroad..." She faltered and swallowed hard. "But Mum said we couldn't afford the fees any more."

Miss Murdoch shook her head; she looked concerned, but also, Beth sensed, curiously relieved too. "You should be having the best tuition now. It's vital not to waste time."

"I know," Beth replied helplessly. There was an awkward silence. Beth looked down at her feet. She watched a long-legged spider lope elegantly over her toe-caps. She wondered, am I right? Is she going to...?

Miss Murdoch suddenly put her hand on Beth's shoulder. It felt heavy and Beth had to steady herself to keep balance. "You and I know," she began, "that music is the most important thing in the world. It should never be stifled by such things as a lack of money. You understand what I mean?" Beth nodded. "And the old have a duty to pass on to the young all that they have learnt. Especially to those who have the gift. I think you have it, Beth, and I want to help you."

Beth felt a sudden spurt of excitement. She was right! This woman was offering her music lessons, she, who had once played in concerts all over the world. She looked into Miss Murdoch's intent face. It was soft, lined, the eyes slightly hooded; there was a hint of suffering there too, even something haunted. "You mean," said Beth slowly, "you're willing to teach me?"

"For nothing," said Miss Murdoch, holding herself very still, as if much hung on Beth's next few words. "Well? Do you like the idea?"

Beth swallowed hard again. Her hands felt clammy and she wiped them surreptitiously on her jeans. This was too good to be true. "I'll have to ask Mum," she said, but she could not help smiling, and they both took this to be the real answer.

"Wonderful," declared Miss Murdoch, pressing her hands together. "It's a long time since I had a pupil of your talent." She seemed genuinely pleased. But then the conversation took a strange turn. The woman put her head slightly to one side and said, "You're just the right age… You are twelve, aren't you? The paper got that right?" Beth nodded, puzzled. "Don't mind my asking. It's just that… Well, you're quite tall for your age, aren't you. And your hair…" She reached out and touched it. "Just the right colour."

"Colour?" Beth echoed, taking a step away. Why had the woman's voice suddenly changed? Something wasn't right here.

Miss Murdoch seemed confused. "I mean," she said, as if laughing it off, "I'm very fond of red hair. Mine was the same colour once, though you would never guess it now, would you?"

But Beth wasn't convinced. Something like a shadow crossed her mind, perhaps a dark premonition of all the trouble that was to flow from this meeting.

Miss Murdoch coughed. "Of course," she murmured, as if half to herself. "You may not, after all, want lessons from an old woman who's living on past triumphs. I will quite understand if you don't."

The subtle threat was enough to jolt Beth out of her doubts. She couldn't let such an opportunity pass just because she felt uneasy. "No," she blurted out, "I'd love to have the lessons. I really need them. I've missed having them so much, you can't begin to guess how much."

"Oh, I think I can." Miss Murdoch smiled. "I shall telephone your mother, then," she added.

"My mother?"

"About the lessons. That is, if you're quite sure you want to go ahead with them."

Beth flashed her a grateful glance. "Of course I do. But I may not be good enough."

"Oh, you'll do, I'm sure," said the woman, and there was such a strange certainty in her voice. Beth shuddered a little.

They moved rapidly in silence down the path until they emerged into the village street. Here Miss Murdoch said, "Now tell your mother about our chat, won't you. And I'll ring her this evening."

Beth wanted to escape now. She gave the briefest of nods and ran off down the street, slowing to a breathless walk once Miss Murdoch was out of sight.

Chapter 2
Daydreams

Beth made her way down the side of the house and sat on a seat in the garden. She could hear her mother working in the kitchen, preparing a business lunch for one of her clients. Beth thought she ought to go in and help her – there had been some vague talk about her helping her mum during the summer holidays – but she felt too agitated by the morning's encounter with Miss Murdoch to think about cooking. She slipped her hands into her pockets and closed her eyes.

She summoned up a familiar dream: her hands flew over the piano keys, the music unfolded with a rapturous tone and perfect timing. By her side was a figure: it was faceless, sexless, insubstantial, but it knew everything about the piano and was her guiding spirit. She tried to superimpose Megan upon that faceless figure, but only a dark shadow appeared, a softly mobile face that would not focus. Beth's apprehension on hearing the stick snap in the wood, and seeing the shadowy figure move through the trees, came back to her and she shivered.

She imagined herself approaching the old house Megan lived in with her sister. (What was her sister's name?) It stood behind tall, ragged hedges that had gaps in them through which she had peered, curious to know what went on in such a mysterious place. A row of windows, some shuttered upstairs, a formation broken only by the imposing front door, looked down darkly at the passer-by.

Beth pictured herself, when much younger, creeping up the drive, watched by a friend. She saw herself knock on the door, two heavy, hollow knocks, and then run away, shrieking, convinced she was about to be pursued by two mad crones. She felt ashamed of this now, but she couldn't help laughing at herself, at the fear which then had seemed so real.

Beth's mother finished piping cream around the raspberry Pavlova and went to the sink to rinse out the piping-bag. Through the window she saw her daughter sitting quietly in the garden with her eyes closed. How like Beth that pose is, thought Mrs Brooke. Half in this world, half somewhere else.

Sitting at the kitchen table that morning, sipping coffee, she had stared at the picture in the newspaper. Her first reaction was one of surprise; then she felt a rare surge of pride. She recalled the concert and the odd, almost anguished feeling when Beth had first stepped up on the stage with the light on her and the crowd clapping. This is my daughter, she'd said to herself, the one that I've nurtured and fought with and kept by my side all this time; yet now, up there, she is a stranger, someone I hardly seem to know. By a familiar train of thought, she went back three years, when Beth and Tim's father had left to set up a business in Australia and had decided not to return. Beth had seemed to take the news better than Tim at first; but now Mrs Brooke had her doubts.

She sighed. Rapping on the window, she succeeded in gaining Beth's attention. "Perfect timing as usual," she said when Beth came in. "I'm just about finished."

"Sorry, Mum. Did I say I was going to help you this morning?"

Her mother shook her head. "What a memory you've got, Beth. You can at least help me to pack up all this food." Together, they began to load the food for the business lunch into large, polystyrene containers.

"Gran'll look in on you this morning, if you're going to be in," Mrs Brooke said.

"Mum, we can look after ourselves," Beth protested, not for the first time.

"Oh, I'm sure you can," her mother said wryly. "But Gran doesn't quite see it that way. Besides…" Mrs Brooke shrugged.

They stacked the containers at the end of the table, then Beth sat down. She saw the local paper folded on the dresser and she wondered whether her mum had seen the picture. She hesitated to find out. But this morning Mrs Brooke, sensing what her daughter was thinking, opened the paper and put it in front of her daughter. "What do you think of that, Beth?"

Beth picked up the paper and said ruefully, "Don't I look dreadful." Staring at the picture, she suddenly realized that what the lens had captured was less her physical likeness, more a central image from her daydreams; that was why she felt so shy about it. "Mum," she began, closing the paper. "I met Miss Murdoch in the woods this morning."

"Miss who?"

"She lives in that big house in Monk's Lane. You must have seen her about."

"Oh, the one who always wears those long coats, no matter what the weather. Strange woman."

Mrs Brooke took the paper and looked at the picture again, hoping to get Beth talking about that. Inwardly, Beth took a deep breath. "Mum," she began again, trying to quell a faint tremor in her voice. "Miss Murdoch has offered to give me piano lessons."

Mrs Brooke looked up from the paper in surprise. "Piano lessons?"

"She was once a famous pianist. Gran knows about her."

"Yes, but…" She bit the words back. She thought about taking hold of Beth's hand – but it had been a long time since she had done that. "Beth, we've talked about all this before. I know business is picking up, I'm getting several bookings a week now, but the bills still need paying off first, and the lessons won't be cheap…" She hated herself for saying this but the words just tumbled out.

Beth cut in, "But these are free."

Mrs Brooke was brought up sharp. "Free?" she echoed. She saw the sudden, burning eagerness in her daughter's eyes. "Are you sure, love?"

Beth nodded eagerly. She recounted the meeting in the woods.

Mrs Brooke remained dubious. "But why? She hardly knows you."

Beth pointed to the paper. "I don't know why they are free," she said, "but there's no reason to say no, is there?"

Mrs Brooke shook her head, but she felt uneasy.

"Please, Mum. She's going to ring you about it this evening."

"I'll think about it," said Mrs Brooke. "Now, my girl, you can help me load this on to the car. I must be off in a few minutes."

The sound of her mother's car drew away; silence closed over the house. It was a silence Beth liked: it gave her the space and freedom to daydream. Once more she looked at herself in the paper and felt again that fierce determination to succeed, to be the focus of all eyes in a hushed hall, pouring out music which said: this is what I am, this is what I feel, this is what makes me different. The strength of such feelings and images frightened her a little: where did they come from? And wasn't it all little more than a fantasy? The school concert had shown her that it wasn't, that she could do it, that she could be a real musician.

She folded the paper and left it on the dresser. She wandered to her piano and played a few bars absent-mindedly. There was a flaw in her dream: she had known it even as she was taking her bow at the concert. This audience may not have noticed, but the pieces she had played were a little too easy, too facile, for someone who wanted to make more than an impression, and she was acutely aware of the passages she hadn't got right. She was developing a talent in a vacuum, that was the problem.

It had not always been so. Before Dad had left – how her life had been divided into two by that event! – there had been lessons every week. She was a "natural", her teacher had said. At first, Dad had continued to send money for the lessons, but this had dried up. Her mother had demanded sacrifices all round and the lessons had ended. She bitterly resented that, but she knew, in the circumstances, she had no choice. She tried not to let her mum see how disappointed she was. The lessons at her new school were good and her teacher gave her more time than she was strictly allowed, but they weren't enough.

In the absence of real progress, her dreams of success grew, they filled her days and nights, gave them a secret excitement which she could not do without.

She began to practise. The easy and facile would not fool Megan.

Would she and the strange woman get on? Could Megan transform her instinctive talent into something disciplined and controlled? Was this to be her lucky day?

Chapter 3
Tim

Tim wandered up the village street towards the baker's where his grandmother worked part time. He was feeling pleased with himself, in particular with his "gut reaction" as he put it on seeing Beth featured in the paper that morning. He had even punched the air with his fist and half-shouted, "Yes," as if watching a goal being scored in a football match. No jealousy, no little threads of envy, that's what pleased him. Throughout his childhood he had watched Beth's struggles with music. She and that old piano that Grandad had bought her not long before he died were inseparable. He saw how the music preoccupied her, how it continued in her mind long after she had left the keyboard, how it had made her different in some essential way from other girls. He felt thankful that he did not have the pressure of such talent himself.

He entered the baker's shop. "Hi, Gran," he called. "Mum's got a lunch to do today and she wants you to look in on us."

"I shan't be long," said Gran. "Here, take this loaf and these rolls. I'll be down in about half an hour." Looking at her tall, thin, pale grandson with his stiff, untidy brown hair, she had a sudden thought: he's going to be just like my brother; but she suppressed the thought almost at once, for her brother had been drowned in the war, barely nineteen years old.

"Gran," said Tim, "I've got a holiday project to do. Can you believe it? It's for Mr Davies."

"Good," said Gran with a smile. She settled on a stool to give her feet a rest. "Keep you out of mischief."

Tim pulled a face. The truth was he was

feeling annoyed at having part of his precious holiday taken up with school work. His instinct was to get it done and out the way as soon as he could. "We've got to study an old house in the village, you know, it's history and that; we've got to present a file on it. It all sounds a bit boring to me."

Gran was not taken in by that; she looked interested. "Have you chosen a house yet?"

Tim shook his head. "I thought you might help me with that. What about your cottage?"

Gran looked dubious. "It goes back a long way," she said, "but I don't think there's much written about it. You'd be better off choosing a more interesting house."

"I'll have to look around then," Tim sighed.

Gran had often in the past helped him with his homework, especially when at primary school he had had trouble learning to read. She was pleased he still occasionally sought her help.

"See you later," he called as he left the shop.

He looked at some of the old buildings in the high street, a jumbled mix of Tudor,

Georgian, Victorian, with a few discreet modern additions. Which one should he choose? And how did you gain entry to such places? Surely you didn't just knock on the door and say, "Hi, can I do a project on your house, please." Did Mr Davies have any idea...? He began to feel daunted by the prospect. Perhaps he should concentrate on the architecture of the house. That way he could use the camera Dad had unexpectedly sent him for his birthday. Pictures of the details, the door-frame, the cornices, the plaster-work and beams, the gables, the crazy way some of the timber-framed buildings leaned...

He found Beth sitting in the dining-room at the piano. She was making no effort to play, just sat there staring at a score. She smiled at him vaguely. "How's the prodigy?" he teased. She stuck out her tongue. Then she swung off the piano stool and sat beside him at the table.

"What do you know about Megan Murdoch?" she asked.

Tim looked surprised. "You mean, that old bat at *Whit's End*?"

"She's not an old bat."

"You used to be terrified of her. And of her sister."

"I was only a kid then."

"Oh, so what are you now? Don't tell me, you're a…"

"You say that again and I'll kick you."

"OK, so what do you want to know about her for?"

"She's going to give me piano lessons."

Tim caught the sudden eagerness in her voice. "Is she? Since when?"

"Since this morning. I met her in the woods. She really scared me at first. She was like a big shadow. I felt like running away from her. Silly, really. But then we got talking. Did you know that she was once a famous pianist?" Tim knew at once that this was, for Beth, the one over-riding fact about Megan Murdoch, the one that eclipsed all others. "She doesn't play much now, she can't, she's got something wrong with her hands." Beth looked at her own hands and winced slightly, remembering the swelling she had seen in Megan's.

"Why you?" Tim asked. "She hardly knows you."

"She read about me in the paper."

"Ah," Tim nodded. "Have you told Mum yet?"

"She said she'd think about it."

Tim laughed and gave her a playful push. "You know what that means," he said. "No mooching about in one of your infuriating daydreams, no humming tunes when you should be doing the hoovering. You'll even have to help with the cooking." Tim knew that Beth hated all such household chores; it was one of his favourite themes.

"I've already offered," she said, pushing back.

"Doesn't she move fast! And what did Mum say to that? Did she faint?"

"I don't think she really believed me," said Beth, grinning.

Tim got up and said, "I'm going to make some coffee. Do you want some?" Beth followed him into the kitchen. It smelt of freshly baked bread. Suddenly, she felt hungry and she cut herself a chunk of the bread to eat with her coffee.

"Are you really going to have lessons, then, with this…?"

"Megan Murdoch. Funny name, isn't it. Yes, I am. Why not?"

Tim shrugged. "It's just that they're a bit weird, aren't they? Living in that ramshackle old house. That Megan in particular."

Beth started to defend them. "Well, her sister's all right…"

Tim pounced on the implication. "But Megan isn't? Got you there."

Beth got up to leave. "Oh, grow up, Tim," she said loftily.

Later that evening Megan telephoned. She had a long conversation with Beth's mother.

"It's all fixed," she said to Beth, who had been sitting on the stairs trying to listen to what they were saying. "You're to have a trial lesson tomorrow."

"Great," exclaimed Beth.

The house settled into its usual routine.

Beth practised on the piano. Mrs Brooke had the portable television on in the kitchen, half-watching it while she worked out menus for future bookings. Tim played a computer game in his room.

Often, before she went to sleep, Beth would scribble music on a score pad. On this particular night she had the sense of a new tune, tantalizing snatches of it, beginning to form in her mind. But whenever she tried to catch it on the score pad, it proved elusive, like water running through her fingers. This left her feeling vaguely frustrated. She tossed and turned for a long while before sleep overcame her.

Chapter 4
The Sisters

Beth arrived early outside the sisters' house. She paced in the shadows of the ragged privet hedge that hid much of the lower part of the house from the street. She felt nervous. A strange feeling came over her, as if she was acting a part, pretending to be someone else. The house loomed in shadow. It had a neglected look, moss grew on the lintels, weed in the gravel. Only the flower borders and the urns were well tended.

The church clock struck ten. Beth walked uncertainly over the gravel drive and up the three steps to the heavy front door. Blue paint flaked around the brass knocker. She knocked twice and listened to the sound echo deep in the house. No one answered. Instead, she heard heavy footsteps on the gravel to her left. As Beth turned with a start, the figure of a stout, elderly woman in trousers and a large jumper came into view. She carried a trowel and she wore muddy boots. Seeing Beth, she stopped and said, "Yes?"

Beth recognized Megan's sister and she suddenly remembered the woman's name: Ivy. "Hello," she answered shyly, coming down the steps. She had seen Ivy many times striding through the village or hurtling around in a battered Range Rover. "I've come for my first lesson." That seemed to puzzle Ivy. She dropped her trowel and stepped closer.

"What lesson?"

Beth felt foolish. She thought, what if this is all just one of my daydreams? She had to control a feeling of panic. She looked at Ivy's enquiring face and she explained, haltingly, about Megan's offer. The old woman's response was curious. She made a strange sound, suggesting impatience, but she did not direct this at Beth. She shook her head and muttered, then made her way up the steps to the front door. There she fumbled for a key in her pocket and inserted it into the lock before turning to Beth and saying with undisguised reluctance, "You'd better come in, then. I'll see if my sister is down yet."

They stepped into a large, dark hall smelling of polished wood. In front of Beth was a flight of stairs branching to the left along the landing; the stair-carpet was threadbare. To the right were two doors, one leading to Ivy's living-room where she spent much of her time watching television, the other to the dining-room and the kitchen beyond that. To the left was an elegantly furnished room used only for visitors and special occasions. Behind that was the music-room where Megan spent much of her time. Light filtered down into the dark hall from the coloured landing window. The only sound was the solemn tick of the grandfather clock beside the front door.

Ivy moved towards the stairs, but then, thinking better of it, she turned and said, "When did my sister make this arrangement with you?" Beth was now feeling even more unsure of herself. She tried to keep her voice steady as she answered. "Yesterday. We met, and then she rang my mother last night."

"And how did she know you were looking for lessons?"

"I wasn't. I mean, I was, but we couldn't afford..." Beth faltered.

"And?" Ivy prompted, frowning.

"Miss Murdoch saw the report in the paper about my performance at the school concert. She offered to give me a trial lesson this morning."

Ivy considered this.

In her embarrassment, Beth said, "Is there anything wrong? I mean, should I come back another time?"

Ivy sighed and shook her head. Her face softened. "No, don't worry. It's just that all this is a surprise to me. My sister didn't mention it. And I'm wondering whether it is wise at the moment. You see, the last pupil she had fell rather seriously ill. Megan got so upset she said she would never have another pupil... Oh, but I shouldn't be telling you this, should I?" She paused and stared up the stairs, lost in thought. Beth felt acutely awkward: what had she walked into?

Ivy turned back to her. "Are you sure that this is what you want?" It sounded like a desperate plea. Beth assumed she was referring to the piano lessons. "Yes," she answered. "I've always wanted to be a piano player, ever since I can remember. But I can't teach myself."

"No, of course not. It's just that…" But Ivy was cut short by the sound of a door opening upstairs. She frowned again and went to the foot of the stairs. "Megan," she called. "You've got a visitor."

Megan glided slowly down the stairs. She paused on the landing to survey the two below. Beth felt a coldness creep up the back of her neck. The sight of Megan, once more a shadowy silhouette, brought back the uneasiness she had felt in the wood the day before.

"Oh," Ivy protested, addressing her sister. "What on earth have you got that old dress on for?" Megan wore a long, olive-green dress shot through with threads of emerald that caught the light as she moved. Watching Megan descend the last steps, Beth once more had the sensation that she was in a dream or a play.

Megan ignored her sister. She approached Beth with a smile and said, "I'm so glad your mother gave permission for you to come, Beth. And I see you've met my sister, Ivy." She scrutinized Beth, putting her hands on the girl's shoulders. "Beth, do you feel all right?"

Beth nodded. "Just a bit nervous," she admitted with an attempt at a laugh.

Megan nodded understandingly. "I'm sure you'll soon feel at home here."

At that, Ivy made a sort of impatient grunt. "Megan," she said, "I'd like a word with you. In private, if I may. I'm sure Beth won't mind waiting." She made her way towards her living-room.

Megan raised her eyebrows and said in an exaggerated whisper to Beth, "Don't mind my sister. She's not as grumpy as she pretends to be. She just doesn't like surprises, that's all. Wait here a moment, will you, while I calm her down."

They closed the living-room door behind them. Beth was alone in the dark hall with the tick of the grandfather clock and the dust swirling in the faint beams from the windows. To the right of the front door was an old leather armchair and she perched on this, wincing slightly at the coldness on her bare legs. She could hear the sisters talking in quick spurts, their voices rising occasionally. She was uncomfortably aware that she was the cause of their argument. The clock struck the quarter hour. It made her jump. She got up and wandered around the hall. The floor-boards creaked, and the sisters paused in their muffled talking as if listening to what she was doing. She froze at the foot of the stairs, the subdued light in her red hair.

The silence, the immobility, seemed to stretch for ever. I must get out of here, Beth said to herself. I should never have come. I'm not wanted. I'm trespassing. None of it feels right. But what her mind told her to do had no effect on her limbs. She continued to stand at the foot of the stairs listening to the sisters' voices. One little dash to the door, that's all it would take. She took a few steps towards it but her limbs felt extraordinarily heavy. By slow degrees, she reached the front door.

No, she could not just run. Think how it would look. What would the sisters say, or her mum, or even Tim? How could she explain how she felt to them?

It was then that she thought she heard another voice. It was just a whisper but she thought it said, "I wish they would stop arguing." Beth shivered. She sat down abruptly on the cold leather armchair. This is not real, she told herself, it's a bad daydream.

Suddenly, the living-room door opened and the sisters came out. Beth saw that Ivy was angry, but when she spoke to the girl she kept her voice under control. "I'm sorry about all this, Beth," she said, "but I expect you'll understand in time." She opened the front door and went outside, banging the door behind her.

Megan looked flushed and uneasy. She walked abstractly around the hall to compose herself. Then she took Beth's hand and said, "My sister's always been like that, ever since we were girls. You mustn't let it bother you. Now, let me show you the music-room."

Beth stopped in the doorway of the music-room and took in the whole, long, cluttered, brilliantly-lit room in one intense impression. There was a strong sense of green, like the light in the wood: the green of the garden glowing through the French windows, the dark, pine-coloured curtains, the pale green damask of the chaise-longue, the huge pot of fern on a cabinet and the leaves entwined in the pattern of the wallpaper. There were signs of habitation – a shawl on a chair, an open book, a stack of scores on the piano, a vase of flowers dropping its petals. Her eyes focused on the grand piano by the French windows, its dark, polished wood reflecting the window frame and the clouds moving in the sky. And she felt such a spurt of intense excitement it was almost like choking. She approached the piano unsteadily, running her hands along it as if to confirm its reality. Turning to Megan, who was watching her from just inside the door, she said, "May I play it?"

Megan nodded. She watched Beth settle before the piano. She grasped the back of a chair to steady herself as Beth ran her fingers up and down the keys. Perhaps this is the girl I've been looking for all my life, Megan said to herself. She listened to the girl's playing. It flowed with a natural fluency and a fine sense of discrimination.

Beth suddenly remembered where she was; she stopped playing. Megan shuddered. "Oh, go on, child. It's beautiful. Don't mind me. Play what you like. I need to know what you can do." Beth thought Megan looked strange, but she had no time to think about this, the piano was demanding all her attention. She played one of her favourite pieces, a sonata by Schubert. The quality of the notes was so different, so much more expressive, than anything she could coax out of her upright piano at home or even the piano at school; it was like discovering the piece of music anew.

Megan sat in a chair and watched her. The pale, serious face, the sprinkling of freckles on the arms, the long, wavy red hair – it was exactly right. Perhaps at last she was to be rewarded for her lifelong search for the right girl.

Beth came to the end of the movement. She looked up at Megan and said, "It's wonderful." As Megan did not immediately respond, she added, "Do I play well enough?"

Megan approached the piano. Her face was animated now, her eyes seemed to glow. "You play extraordinarily well, Beth, far better than I had hoped. But there are many things to learn too, I'm sure you know that." Beth nodded eagerly. "We shall work well together, I am convinced of that. Everything feels right to me."

Beth's confidence flooded back. She launched into another piece. When she had finished, Megan pointed out ways of rephrasing some of the passages, altering the tempo here, the volume there. Beth absorbed all the information hungrily; at last she was learning again!

Soon after midday, Ivy appeared at the door

and interrupted them. "Megan," she boomed. "I think you've worked that child hard enough for one morning. We don't want to make her ill, do we?" She disappeared before Megan could respond.

Her words had a curious effect on her sister. Megan became uncertain and nervous. The change was so quick that Beth rose from the piano stool and asked clumsily, "Are you all right, Megan?"

Megan shook her head as if to clear it. "Of course, my dear," she said. "Just a little tired all of a sudden. I think I got carried away. You must be feeling tired too. I hope I haven't worked you too hard."

"I've loved every minute of it," Beth said with conviction.

They chatted for a few more minutes. Then, as Beth was about to leave, she caught sight of a little painted portrait of a girl. It stood on a writing table in a silver frame. Without thinking about it, she picked it up. "Who's this?" she asked. The girl looked a little like Beth: she was about the same age, tall, pale, with long, wavy hair that had a strong reddish tinge. She looked sad, though; instinctively, Beth felt sorry for her.

Megan took the picture from her and said, "She was an ancestor of mine. She lived in this house just before the first world war. She was very musical too. That's why I like to have her portrait here. The poor girl died young, I'm afraid; she was never well. I have a feeling that this room was her favourite place in this house." She replaced the picture on the writing table. They continued to stare at it. Suddenly, Beth felt a vague, cold sensation of fear; her hands curled into fists and she turned towards the door. Megan seemed to notice this. Quickly, she said, "You'll come again soon? Shall we say the day after tomorrow?"

Beth nodded slowly. She walked towards the door, pausing to take a long, last look at the music-room.

Outside, the light was almost blinding. Even when her eyes had grown accustomed to it, the familiar world of the village seemed strange now, oddly unreal, as if she did not quite belong to it any more.

Megan stood at the window in the hall and watched her go. "At last," she whispered to herself, "at last." Then she returned to the music-room, sat down on the chaise-longue and said, as if to the air, "Well, Helen, what do you think?"

Chapter 5
Gran

An idea came to Gran when she woke and, after breakfast, she climbed the stairs to the attic. It was full of things she could not bear to throw away. After a lot of rummaging around, she found what she was looking for: a large wooden chest which contained a stack of old photograph albums. Gran looked through them until she found the two that she had in mind.

She was sitting on the settee browsing through one of them when Tim came in. His camera dangled ostentatiously from his neck. "Hi, Gran," he said. "What have you got there?" Gran motioned him to sit beside her.

She pointed to a small brown picture of a large house and said, "Do you recognize that place? The picture was taken by your great-great-uncle Harry in 1910."

Tim was surprised to discover he was looking at a version of *Whit's End*. "That's funny," he said. "I've just been talking about this place with Beth. It's a bit creepy, isn't it?"

"I've never been inside it," said Gran. "The two women who live there don't mix much. But why were you talking about it?"

"Beth's going there for piano lessons. Hasn't she told you?"

Gran shook her head, baffled. "I've heard nothing about it."

Tim mentally kicked himself. He suddenly remembered that Mum told him not to say anything about it to Gran yet – something about "old people not liking anything that looks like charity". But it was too late now; he told her what he knew. "She's really taken with that Megan," he added. "Never stops talking about her."

Gran stared at the album, thinking.

"Don't you think it's a good idea?"

"Well, Ivy's all right, I suppose. But I've always had my doubts about Megan. She's never been quite right, if you know what I mean." Gran shook her head slowly. "Oh, well, I suppose I'd better keep my nose out of it," she sighed.

"She'll be all right," Tim said. "She was desperate to have music lessons again; you know Beth."

Gran turned a page of the album and they looked at the sepia pictures in silence for a while.

"Now, Tim" said Gran. "You were asking about a a house for your project and I suddenly thought of *Whit's End*."

"Because you had all these pictures?"

Gran pointed to a picture of a gardener. "That's your great-great-uncle Harry. He was the head gardener there, I think, when this was taken. He was a dab-hand with the camera, too, quite a hobby of his, I believe."

Tim's interest quickened. He leafed through the album, listening to Gran's explanations. "That's your great-great-aunt Minnie. She was the housekeeper then. Later they got married and came to live in this cottage." Under each picture was a little caption written in a shaky copperplate, giving dates, locations, names. For 1911 there was a group portrait showing Mr and Mrs Murdoch, their daughter Helen aged 11, and the governess, Miss Marshall. They were posing stiffly on some garden steps, each in dark, sombre clothes except for Helen who wore a long, light-coloured dress.

"That girl," said Tim, pointing, "looks a bit like Beth, doesn't she."

Gran peered down her bifocals. "There's a bit of a resemblance. She does look rather serious, doesn't she. They all do." Gran paused, reminded of something. "There's a story about that girl, if I remember. She died young, I think..." She shook her head doubtfully.

Tim picked up the other album. "This is great, Gran. With all this stuff on *Whit's End*, it'll be dead easy to do my project."

"Well, that's the idea," said Gran. "But you'll have to get permission from those sisters. I'm not sure they'll welcome a boy poking around their house."

"Beth'll help me. I'll get her to ask them."

When Tim had left, Gran returned to the attic and turned over the albums in the trunk until she found what she was looking for. It was great-aunt Minnie's diary, a thick grey book written in fading brown ink. The old lady had always been telling far-fetched stories of ghosts and hauntings at *Whit's End*. Gran brought the book downstairs. She strained her eyes trying to read Minnie's wayward handwriting. Opening it at random, she read, *I'm sure the child's not well. Her cough quite gives me the shivers. But no one will take any notice of me if I mention it, her mother's too wrapped up in her own illnesses and Miss Marshall just stares at me with her governessy eyes, making me feel that it's none of my business. And I daren't mention it to the Master. Perhaps I'm making too much of it...*

Gran studied a photograph of Helen and she thought she saw why the housekeeper was concerned – the thin, pale face, the shadows under the eyes. A little further on she read, *I saw, this morning, from an upstairs window,*

Helen hiding in the shrubbery while Miss Marshall was calling for her. She should have been in her lessons. But when the Master came out, he didn't have to say a word, she just crept out and went to him, hanging her head. I think she really fears him. Sometimes he's so cold and angry with her. I don't know why, she's his only child, you'd think he would adore her, especially with his wife always on her sickbed. Cook thinks it's all because the Mistress has never been right since the girl was born. He blames the child for her illnesses. Surely he couldn't be so monstrous, I said to Cook, but she's known them longer than I have. It's so unfair on the child, she's such a sweet little thing...

Gran turned the page and read the next entry. *He seems to think it's so important that she plays well, like a real professional. And she does. It's a real joy to hear. Now the child's got it into her head to play the piano in church. She wants to play something that she's written herself, she says. Who ever heard of a child doing that? But for once her father has said yes, and I think he's silly to do so. Can't he see that the strain of such a thing will be too much for the girl? She gets so excitable and then her cough comes on. If I were him, I'd pack her off to a nursing home. I've tried to warn Miss Marshall about it but that hoity-toity governess said to me, "If you try and interfere, Minnie, you'll be out on your ear. Believe me, I know." And I have to admit she's right.*

Gran read on. After a while a sense of sadness, of foreboding, came over her. It was clear that the girl was doomed, but why were they all, apart from Minnie, so blind to the danger? She closed the diary, unable to read on, and sat thinking of Helen. Then into her mind came Beth. Beth was walking up to *Whit's End*, she was knocking on the door, and it was Great-Aunt Minnie who was opening the door and ushering her in. Gran shook her head. She decided to go for a brisk walk to dispel her mood.

Leaning against a stile to get her breath back, she saw Megan Murdoch striding across the field towards the wood. The woman's old-fashioned grey coat flapped in the wind. Gran watched her disappear into the trees. She was about to walk there too, but the thought of meeting Megan put her off. Why did that woman make her feel so uneasy?

Chapter 6
Spectral Music

Beth's sleep had been full of strange, jumbled pictures, of faces peering at her, of wanderings through a vast and dark house; she was searching for something but for what she could not tell. She woke feeling as if she had been on a long and frustrating journey. When she came into the kitchen, Tim said, "You look rough. Bad dreams?" She shook her head, unnerved at his guess.

The music-room that morning had a soft green light. It was silent, sealed off from the outside world. As Beth stepped into it and stood by the door looking about her, she had the curious sense that the room held a secret. The feeling was so powerful that, as she wandered about the room, listening to Ivy's receding footsteps and waiting for Megan to come, her senses became finely attuned. She listened, but for what she could not say. She walked nervously to the piano. Her reflection in the wood reminded her of the portrait of the girl, but it was no longer on the writing table. She could not see it anywhere. Sitting at the piano, she thought of the girl, the intense eyes, the white face. She looked through the French windows. There was a breeze; the trees and the bushes were agitated. She watched their silent movement. Vague images of her dream of the night before came back to her. Then she caught sight of something white. It was like the glimpse of a dress moving behind a bush.

The silence was extraordinary.

Then she heard the haunting music for the first time. It was so faint that at first she thought it was a tune in her head. Such tunes came to her out of nothing, often difficult to recapture later on the piano. But this music continued without a break. It was a sonata.

Quiet. Intense. But with little skittish movements – like a child skipping through a graveyard. It stopped before the first movement was half way through. Beth yearned for the next part. She tried to continue it in her head. Then she tried to reproduce some of it on the piano.

She heard voices in the hall, Ivy and Megan's. They were arguing about something again. Was it about her?

Megan entered, smiling a little thinly. She wore a grey skirt, a cardigan, with several strings of amber-coloured beads over a white blouse. She insisted on kissing Beth. The girl noticed her make-up and heavy perfume. Megan was eager to talk of her plans for the piano lessons. Putting a score on the piano, she said, "I know you like Chopin, so let's work on this piece this morning. It was one of the first I performed as a girl. It's always been a favourite with my pupils."

They worked hard. The grandfather clock struck midday before they became aware of how much time had passed. Megan said, "Goodness, we have done well. I think we deserve some coffee, don't you?" She went out. Beth felt satisfied with her performance, even though she was surprised at how many small faults and weak interpretations Megan was able to point out.

But she was exhausted too. The restless night she had had, and the intense concentration needed that morning, had strained her nerves. She sat quietly with her hands in her lap, aware again of the peculiar silence of the room. Faint strains of the mysterious music came back to her.

Megan returned with the coffee. Taking her cup, Beth asked about the music she had heard. "It was so quiet," she said. "I thought I was imagining it; but I could never have thought up something so beautiful..." She faltered. Her words were having a strange effect on Megan. The woman put her cup down unsteadily. She ran a hand over her face, then she said, with repressed excitement, "Are you sure you heard this?"

Suddenly Beth felt scared of her. It was the same feeling that she had had on encountering Megan in the wood. She nodded warily.

Megan got up slowly, her hands clasped tightly. She stood by the French windows. Beth thought she heard her muttering, "So soon..." What was going on? Without turning, Megan said, "I think it's time for you to go now, Beth."

Beth jumped up guiltily. "Yes, of course, Megan," she mumbled. "I'm sorry." She felt bewildered at being dismissed in this way, particularly when the morning had gone so well. As she reached the door, Megan suddenly turned to her and called, with a note of anxiety, "You will come again soon, won't you?"

"Of course I will. You know how much I love these lessons. Will Saturday be all right?"

Megan nodded, smiled at her briefly, then turned back to look out of the window. Beth crept out, closing the door behind her.

In the shadowy hall Beth was intercepted by Ivy. "Are you all right, Beth?" she asked, studying the girl's puzzled face. Beth nodded politely. "Well, you don't look it. Come in here."

Beth followed her into Ivy's living-room. It

was so different from the music-room that Beth found it hard to believe both rooms could be in the same house. The furniture was plain, modern, rather worn. On the television set was a collection of thimbles, and beside it was a small bookcase full of paperbacks. Magazines were stacked on the floor, and a pair of muddy boots stood on a newspaper just inside the door. There were pot-plants everywhere.

"Now, how are you getting on with my sister?" Ivy asked.

"Very well," said Beth; but as Ivy looked doubtful, she added, "I'm certainly learning a lot from her."

"Good," said Ivy, studying her closely. "And she hasn't upset you at all?"

Beth tried to hide her confusion. She shook her head.

"Well, if she does…" Ivy said. Then she smiled. "I'm so glad it's going well. Now, I wonder if you would like to look around the house before you go? I don't suppose Megan has shown you around, has she?"

They climbed the creaking stairs and

entered a long, dim, wood-panelled passage lined with dark oil-paintings. Beth was shown bedrooms and the bathroom which had an old bath on lion's feet. She was shown little rooms that had no particular purpose, and vast cupboards. It was like her dream-journey through a dark house the night before. Ivy opened a door at the foot of a little passage-way, releasing a musty smell and a sense of cobwebs, dust and neglect. "I don't think I'll take you up there," she chuckled. "This door used to terrify me as a child. Whenever Megan wanted to get her way, she would threaten to open this door and let out the ghost and spirits; and for years I believed her. Even now, I can't bring myself to go up there without a shudder."

Beth, with the haunting music still in her mind, had been on the look-out for a record, tape or CD player on which it might have been played, but all she had seen was a portable radio in what she took to be Ivy's bedroom. Perhaps it had come from that?

Back in the hall, Beth asked, "Shall I say goodbye to Megan?"

Ivy shook her head. "You run along now, Beth. Megan likes to rest after a lesson. We won't bother her now. When are you next due?"

"Saturday."

Ivy opened the door for her, and as Beth stepped down on to the gravel, Ivy called, "And remember, Beth, when you've had enough, don't hesitate to say so. Sometimes my sister presses her pupils too hard."

Arriving home, Beth found the house empty. She knew Tim was supposed to be around to keep an eye on her, but they had a tacit agreement that this was not necessary so long as Mum did not find out. She sat in the garden and turned over in her mind all the impressions she had gained of *Whit's End*. She tried to recall the sonata fragment that, by some inexplicable means, she had heard, but it had gone. Instead, vividly, she recalled the flash of white, like a girl's dress, moving through the windswept leaves.

Tim said to her, "I want you to do me a favour, Beth," and he told her of his plans to use *Whit's End* as the focus of his school project.

"I might," she teased. She wondered whether she really wanted him there, clumping about the house with his camera, distracting everyone. *Whit's End* was so different from home, it was like her own private world. Then she remembered the moments when she had been scared, had felt alone, unprotected; it might be good to have him there after all. "All right," she said. "I'll ask. But I think you'd better phone them too."

"Thanks," said Tim.

That night Beth went to bed early. She knew she was overtired; she prayed for a good night's sleep. She closed her eyes, and in the dark she saw a girl in a white dress skipping among gravestones, and the girl was humming the music Beth had heard so hauntingly in the music-room that day.

Chapter 7
The Score

Saturday. Beth was watching the clock impatiently; she had been ready for her lesson since eight-thirty. She practised for a while until Tim complained of the noise. Then she tried to read a book until her mother demanded help in the kitchen.

"Looking forward to it?" her mother asked.

"Of course," Beth answered warily.

"You think Megan's a good teacher?"

Beth nodded, half-smiled.

"You don't seem too sure."

Beth shook her head. "It's just that I've got so much to learn. I didn't realize how much."

"And you think she's the one to teach you?"

"Mum, why all these questions?"

Her mother shrugged her shoulders. "Oh, it's just that Gran doesn't seem to approve of Megan Murdoch. I don't really know why. Village gossip, I suppose."

"Megan's all right," Beth declared fiercely.

Her mother looked at her curiously. "Well, we needn't take too much notice of Gran. As long as you're happy. I was wondering whether we should offer Miss Murdoch some money. I know I said I couldn't afford it, but…"

"Oh, Mum," Beth protested. "She wouldn't take it."

Mrs Brooke looked sceptical. "She really does it for love?"

"I suppose so," Beth shrugged.

This time, when Beth entered the music-room, Megan was already at the piano, impatient to begin. She studied Beth sharply at first, and then seemed satisfied. They went straight into the lesson and worked so hard even the refreshments Ivy brought in mid-morning were barely touched. At the end of one particularly well-played piece, Megan dropped her usual reserve and cried excitedly, "That was marvellous, Beth," and hugged her awkwardly.

Then Beth was alone in the room. Megan had gone to prepare some lunch. Ivy had gone out. Everything was quiet. She was feeling drained, empty, light, as if she had shed some weight or difficulty. She wandered around the room until she came to the writing table. On it was some music paper. She sat and stared at it. Then she heard the haunting music again. It was like a whisper at first; she strained to hear it. It grew a little louder, although it was never more than faint. She closed her eyes. The music took hold of her, claiming all her attention. As she listened she imagined the notes forming on the staves. What a wonderful piece of music, she thought.

The music faded rather than stopped. She supposed she had heard most of the first movement. The silence after it was almost painful.

Without thinking about it, Beth picked up

the pen on the table and began to write down the music. She wrote with surety and speed. The music echoed in her head and she caught it on the paper without any of the usual hesitations and revisions. One page was filled, then another. She was well into the fourth when Megan came in, carrying a tray of sandwiches and drinks.

The music stopped in Beth's mind. She became aware of Megan's voice, of the tray being placed on the coffee table, of books being moved out of the way. Megan was saying, "I'm sorry it took so long. I had to sort out something with Ivy." She paused. "Are you all right, Beth? You look so pale." Beth rose, rubbed her eyes, managed a smile, and said, "It's probably hunger, Megan. I've never felt so hungry in my life." They ate in silence for a while. Then Megan asked, "What were you doing when I came in just now?"

"I was writing some music," Beth answered, her heart suddenly beating fast.

"Oh, yes, you told me you composed. Can I see what you have written?" Megan rose and brushed some crumbs from her skirt.

Beth felt apprehensive. She said reluctantly, "It's not something I've composed. It's something I've heard, at least I think I have..." She paused. Megan looked at her with a new interest. "And what have you heard?" she asked; she seemed very eager to know.

Beth became tongue-tied. She had a feeling she was sailing into strange water. But if she could not talk to Megan about it, who else could she talk to?

At that moment the telephone rang. They both started. Megan sighed, irritated, then left the room.

Beth returned to the score on the writing table. She stared at it as if seeing it for the first time. She was amazed. It looked nothing like any score she had ever written herself. Her own notation was usually untidy, scribbly, tentative, but this was neat, definite, like a fair copy. Perhaps that was what it was... But no, this was written by someone else. She picked up the top sheet, then let it drop again as if it had scorched her. She stared at it, baffled and disturbed.

She heard Megan replace the receiver and

walk back across the hall. Beth hurriedly resumed her seat. Her heart was pounding erratically.

Megan seemed slightly puzzled. "That was your brother on the telephone," she said. "He asked if he might do a school project on this house. Did you know about this, Beth?"

"Oh, yes. He asked me to mention it. Do you mind?"

"As long as he does not disturb us. I've asked him to ring Ivy later. She deals with that sort of thing. Now, show me what you were composing."

Slowly, Beth fetched the score. She handed it to Megan and went and stood by the French windows. Her heart was still beating uncomfortably fast. There was a minute or so of tense silence. Beth stole a glance at Megan. She had her eyes closed, the score was resting on her lap. Her head was quivering slightly. She seemed so withdrawn. Beth felt alarm. She took a step towards the woman and whispered, "Megan?" but there was no response. Several more agonizing seconds passed. Then Beth panicked. She had never seen anyone like this before. She edged out of the room.

But in the dim, ticking hall, she stopped to reflect. Should she wait to say goodbye? No. As the grandfather clock struck the hour, she knew she did not have the nerve to stay in the house any longer. She let herself out.

Standing at the foot of the steps, she thought: I'm learning again. I'm learning so much. Megan may be strange but she's my best teacher yet. It's wonderful. She says I can be a concert pianist. And that's what I'm going to be.

She did not feel like going home just then... As she wandered to the gate, curiosity directed her steps around to the side of the house where she had never been before. At the back was a Victorian conservatory leaning against the wall; it was in a poor state of repair with glass missing and rust everywhere. Steps led down from the conservatory door; to the left of them were the French windows of the music-room. Beth kept clear of this, not wanting to attract Megan's attention. She followed a path down through the unkempt grass to the shrubbery. Moving around this, she came to an enclosed space, at the end of which was a dilapidated wooden summer house. Inside it was a garden seat.

Beth was not expecting to find this hidden garden. She was intrigued by it. Someone was taking care of it, it looked neat, there were roses, ferns and flowering beds. It was a sun trap, too. Beth went into the little summer-house and sat on the seat. The sun, when free of scudding clouds, shone directly on her. She closed her eyes. The light playing on her closed eyelids gave sensations of colour and movement. She tried to follow the patterns that unfolded and faded in her mind.

Slowly, she became aware of changes within and around her. First, she felt her body temperature change, just as it did with 'flu: hot one minute, shivering the next. She felt the air grow still and cold around her. Then the sounds of the garden began to fade, as if she was going deaf. But she could not move; there was no escape from this.

In a spasm of panic, she forced her eyes

open. The light was dazzling.

Then she felt an acute sense of apprehension. Something was happening. It looked as if the air was coalescing in front of her. A semi-opaque, wavering form, the shape of a girl, was struggling barely three feet away – yes, struggling, as if the ghost – what else could it be? – was attempting to break through an invisible film of air.

Through her fear, Beth recognized the girl, the long hair, the white dress – but not the deathly pallor, the hollow, imploring eyes, the look of exhaustion. Girl and ghost stared at one another, into one another. There was no sound. The ghost drifted closer and raised a hand. Beth felt the touch of burningly cold fingers on her lips and of an icy shimmering that went right through her. Her body reacted with spasmodic movements, and it was this, perhaps, that broke the momentary spell. The ghost's surface suddenly swirled, shifting and curling in agitation; it was as if she was being called away, against her will. Her outline bled slowly into the air.

The bushes hissed in the background. Birds

sung piercingly. Beth stared at the patch of grass where the ghost had been. She clasped her arms tightly around her body and tried to control her shivering.

Gathering her courage, she edged out of the enclosed garden and ran. She ran all the way home, blindly, in a state of barely controlled panic. What had she seen? What had touched her?

There was no one at home. She threw herself on her bed and curled up, panting, still feeling cold; she held still until her pulse slowed down. Had she seen a ghost? It seemed too fantastic. And yet... The face was the same as the girl in the little portrait... No, it must have been some ghastly trick of the light, or of her mind... She lay like that for a long time until she felt calm. She looked at her tense face in the mirror. "You did see a ghost," she said to her image. "You know you did. And she wants something from you."

She heard her mother's car enter the drive. Thankfully, she ran downstairs to greet her, resolutely pushing from her mind such unreal, such frightening thoughts. After all, it was not something Mum would understand. Silly, really…

But in bed that night, Beth was afraid to close her eyes in the dark. When she did so, she heard the mysterious music very far off, as if played in some deep, cavernous place. She felt, too, the ghost's dark, imploring eyes boring into her. Hot and restless, she got up and wandered through the house in her pyjamas. She went out into the moonlit garden.

She said aloud, as if belatedly addressing the ghost, "Who are you? What do you want of me?"

Behind her came a voice. She was seized with terror.

But it was only Tim. "Beth? What are you doing?"

"You nearly frightened me to death," she complained, breathless.

"Me frighten you? How do you think I felt? I thought someone had broken in."

He saw in the moonlight the strained look on her face. "Beth," he said, approaching her with concern. "Are you all right?"

Beth nodded. She took hold of her brother's arm.

"What were you saying just now when I came out?"

"Don't ask," said Beth hoarsely. She wanted to tell Tim about it, but how could she put into words something she hardly understood herself?

They went back inside. Tim watched Beth climb the stairs. She turned briefly at the top to give him a weak, thankful smile. He stayed in the kitchen for a while, sipping a glass of milk. Was Beth sleepwalking? He knew that at times she could act strangely, but until now he hadn't been aware that she was a night prowler. He finished his milk, climbed the stairs and paused outside his mother's room. Luckily she had slept through it all. Now wide awake himself, he tried to read for a bit, but the recollection of Beth's scared face in the moonlight kept troubling him. Coming back from a trip to the bathroom, he noticed that Beth's light was still on. He knocked on her door, softly. Beth did not answer. He supposed she had fallen asleep with the light on. He edged open the door and peered in.

She was sitting at her desk. In front of her was a sheet of music paper, cast in a pool of light, on which she was writing music. She did not look at him, or acknowledge his presence, she just carried on writing. He was fascinated by the smooth, determined way the pen worked across the staves.

"Beth?" he whispered at last. "What are you writing?"

Then slowly she turned to him. Her face was like a mask, thin and white. Her eyes were dark, hollow and glittering, as cold as ice. She looked at him, or rather, through him. Tim shuddered. He tried to say, "What's happened to you?" but the question died in his throat. Her eyes horrified him. He dropped his gaze. Slowly, Beth turned back to her writing and the pen continued its smooth progress across the page.

Chapter 8
Fear

Beth stayed in bed for most of that Sunday morning. Her head ached, she felt unwell. Her mother gave her some aspirin and made a fuss of her until Beth told her to go away.

Late that afternoon, Tim found her in the front room staring out of the window. It was not like her to sit and do nothing. "What were you doing out there last night?" he asked, wanting to find some rational explanation for what he had seen.

Beth gave a weary shake of the head. "I don't remember much about it. I remember you coming out and giving me a fright. Then

I went upstairs … and I suppose I must have gone to sleep." Her brow wrinkled in doubt.

Tim's face expressed disbelief. "You were composing last night when I looked in. Are you saying you were doing that in your sleep?"

Beth frowned at him. "Composing? I went to sleep."

"Have it your own way," Tim shrugged. If she wanted to be mysterious, then let her; why should he care? But she was getting up, a curious look on her face. "What have I said?" Tim muttered as he watched her hurry from the room. He followed her. Upstairs, she opened her score pad and stared at the first page of the music she had written the night before. It was the first movement of the sonata she had heard in the music-room. But, again, it wasn't written in her hand. "That's it," said Tim. "That's what you were writing last night." Beth looked at him in bewilderment. He added more quietly, "It's not written in your usual style, is it?"

Beth shook her head. Why couldn't she remember writing it?

"Then, why…?"

"I don't know." Beth closed the score. Sitting on the bed, she said, "Unless it's…"

Tim waited. "It's … what?" he prompted, baffled. She did not answer. He shifted uneasily by her desk. All at once he began to feel that his little sister, whom he had always sought to protect – especially since Dad had left – was slipping away from him, becoming a stranger.

Suddenly, Beth blurted out, "Do you believe in ghosts?" It was such an unexpected question, Tim laughed. "Of course not," he replied without thinking. "What brought that up?"

"Oh, nothing," she said, clamming up.

He regretted his response. "Come on," he said coaxingly. "Why do you ask?" He could see her struggling to say something, but she shook her head. He asked, without reflection, "Have you seen one? At *Whit's End*?"

Beth nodded uncertainly. "I think so. But I can't be sure. Perhaps not… There was a girl, like me, in a white dress, in the garden. I saw her for a minute… At least, I think I did."

Beth shuddered. "She was scary. I felt so cold, so cut off. In a silent world. And her eyes frightened me, they were so dark and hollow…" Beth dropped her head, overcome with emotion. "Her face," she whispered, "her skin, it was so white, so shifting, like thick mist. And she touched my lips." She felt her lips, then, recalling the cold, shimmering waves that had gone right through her, then covered her face with her hands.

Tim feared she might be about to cry – that was something he always found difficult to handle. "Are you sure about this, Beth?" he said, aware of his own inadequacy. "I mean, it wasn't just some kind of nightmare? Or perhaps it was a real girl, playing in the garden when she shouldn't." Beth made no reply. "I mean, Beth, you're talking about a real ghost here?"

Abruptly, Beth seized the score pad and thrust it into Tim's hands. "But this isn't my writing, is it?" she said vehemently. Tim compared Beth's previous scores with the one she had been writing last night. The difference was uncanny. "I don't understand this," he muttered. A cold, prickly feeling crept through his scalp. He recalled Beth's mask-like face and glittering eyes, and he began to feel afraid himself.

A few days passed. Nothing out of the ordinary happened. Beth slept heavily and dreamlessly. She began to doubt the vision of the ghost; perhaps it had only been a nightmare. It was only the score that continued to trouble her. She had tucked the score pad underneath some other books in her desk drawer and had not dared to take it out. Tim had made a few half-hearted attempts to raise the subject of the ghost again but her reluctance was so evident he grew silent.

They had arranged to return to *Whit's End* together. Beth had toyed with the idea of not returning to the house at all – for fear she might encounter the ghost again – but as the days passed her need for the lessons became so strong her fears were overcome; and with Tim there, she'd feel safer.

Once in the house, they separated. Tim went into the dining-room with Ivy. After some initial suspicion, Ivy had become quite enthusiastic about Tim's request to do a project on *Whit's End*. On the table she had laid out some of the family's archives – albums, account books, certificates, medals, deeds, anything she could lay her hands on; she relished the chance to talk about her family's history.

Beth breathed in the strange atmosphere of the music-room. She smiled nervously at Megan, who was flicking through a score, and said, "What shall we play today?"

"Let's try this," Megan said, showing a score. "What do you think?"

Beth looked at it. It was not one she knew. The challenge excited her. "Great," she said, and they worked steadily on it for the next hour and a half. Beth was ready to finish then, but Megan said, "Just a half an hour more. There's something else I would like you to run through. It'll help me to plan our next lesson. Now, where is it?" She searched through the pile of scores on the piano and another on the writing table. "I think it must be upstairs," she said and she left the room.

Beth was alone in the music-room again. She felt the atmosphere change. It changed so quickly she looked around in fear, half-expecting to see someone else there. The room grew colder.

The garden was very still that day, no sunlight, no breeze, just grey light on the lawn and pale shadows in the leaves. Beth looked through the window at the spot where she thought she had seen the flash of white a few days ago. She now knew that, beyond the shrubbery, was the hidden garden with its little summerhouse, where she had seen...

To distract herself, she went over to the writing table. She opened a drawer. Inside it was the score she had begun to transcribe so mysteriously on her last visit. Gingerly, she took it out. The handwriting was exactly the same as in the score she had written a few nights before in her bedroom; but the fact no longer seemed surprising now. And a thought suddenly came to her: why not play it? At the piano, she had to calm herself: her heart beat fast and her fingers were not steady. She began to play. She found at once that she did not really have to look at the score. Her fingers *knew* what to play. She let the music unfold by itself.

She was aware of a tension building up inside her as she played. It rose in her throat and threatened to choke her. She had to stop playing and gasped to get her breath back. She sat thinking: why do I feel like this? What brought this on?

Then a disturbance in the air outside caught her eye and she stiffened. Through the window she saw the shimmering ghost-girl again. It was like a swirl of dark mist hovering above the grass. The ghost appeared to be clapping, her indistinct hands moving back and forth in the air. There was something wholly unnerving about that silent clap. Beth wanted to scream. The ghost glided slowly towards her, a shimmer of blue in her frosty hair.

Beth managed to close her eyes. She wanted to run but she was incapable of any movement. Then her hands were lifted by an unseen force. They began to play the sonata again. She played like an automaton until she came to the end of the part she had already transcribed. At that point her fingers went limp and she opened her eyes.

As the scream in her throat gathered to bursting point, she was aware of two fleeting images. The first was that the lawn was now empty. The second was of Megan standing in the doorway staring at her intently.

Tim and Ivy were examining the house-keeper's accounts for 1889 when they were startled by a piercing scream from another part of the house. "That's Beth," Tim said in alarm. He raced into the hall and saw Beth burst from the music-room. She careered wildly towards the front door, scrabbling frantically to get it open.

"Beth, what's the...?"

But she had wrenched the door open. She skidded down the steps and flew over the gravel, leaving Tim standing with his mouth open in amazement.

Chapter 9
The Diary

Beth did not return home that day until mid-afternoon. She had been roaming the woods, she said, but Tim, who had gone to look for her there, had not been able to find her, and he was puzzled. She looked completely washed out and her mother, regarding her in dismay, insisted on her going to bed at once.

She hardly slept all night.

The following day she had a headache so bad each movement was painful. Tim was desperate to talk to her about what had happened. Both sisters rang to ask how she was. Her mother became alarmed. "What's going on up there?" she demanded of Tim.

"Beth looks like death and I can't get a word out of her. Do you know?" Tim shrugged. His mother was the last person, he thought, who would believe Beth had seen a ghost, but he gave it a try. "She thinks the place is haunted," he said.

"Haunted?" his mother butted in. The derision in her voice was as much as Tim had expected. He shrugged again. "You can do better than that," she said.

"Perhaps Megan works her too hard," he tried. "Or scares her."

Mrs Brooke considered this: it was something she could comprehend. "Well," she said darkly, "if it goes on, I shall have to put my foot down."

Later, Tim went to see Beth. Lying in semi-darkness, she winced when he opened the door, letting in the light. "Do you want to talk about it?" he asked, but she didn't answer. He sat on the bed. "Beth, we've always shared things."

"Go away, Tim," she whispered. "My head hurts too much."

"Please, Beth."

She seemed touched at last by his concern. Struggling to sit up, she said, "I saw her again. The ghost. She was outside. She began to clap. It was horrible." She stared at Tim in despair. "Why me?" she whispered. "Why is she picking on me?"

But she slept heavily that night; and apart from a stuffiness in her head, she was fine the next day. She went swimming with Tim; and then they decided to visit Gran.

They found Gran sitting at the table with a friend, Mrs Hurst. She was a small, sparse woman with alert eyes behind heavy-rimmed spectacles. The two women were studying a large chart. It was a plan of the church fête showing which stall went where and who was in charge of each. Gran and Mrs Hurst were on the fête's planning committee.

Mrs Hurst made a great fuss of Beth. The reason for this soon became clear. She had a plan which brought a sudden light into Beth's eyes. She said, "We read with great interest the report in the paper about the school concert. You made such an impression, Beth, I did so wish I'd been there myself. Anyway, someone on the committee suggested that we should put on a concert in the church this year, in the evening after the fête. And when we talked about who might play for us, your name was on everyone's lips. Would you like to play for us?"

Beth did not hesitate. "I'd love to," she cried excitedly. Then she was assailed by the familiar nerves.

"Think about it first," said Gran.

"Do you mean the whole concert?" asked Tim.

"Of course not," Mrs Hurst laughed. "Although I'm sure Beth could manage that quite well. No, just the second half. We've already got a singer and a harp player."

"Beth'll think about it and let you know," said Gran, giving her a proud smile.

"We've got a good piano in the church, you know," Mrs Hurst added.

"Yes, I know," said Beth. "I've tried it."

Tim went into the living-room. There was

something he wanted to check in one of Gran's old photograph albums. He sat on the settee with the album and turned to the pictures for 1912 which showed Helen Murdoch. Tim studied them carefully. The soft brown sepia gave the girl a serene, beautiful, but almost unreal look. Most of the pictures were taken about the house or snapped in the conservatory, the summer house and the garden. In some Helen was flanked by her parents and grandparents, her governess, other relatives, but there was a group of pictures in which Helen appeared only with her father. He always stood behind her, tall, bearded, unsmiling; in these pictures the girl seemed tense, stiff, and troubled. Tim turned the page. For a while he did not understand what he was looking at. All the Murdochs were there, with their servants, a priest and other mourners, swathed in black. They were processing after a coffin. But no Helen. Suddenly, Tim realized that what the pictures showed were dim, shadowy moments of Helen's own funeral.

He was thinking, is this who Beth has been

seeing? when she came in. She was full of suppressed excitement about the concert. "I've said yes," she declared. "I really don't need to think about it." She saw that Tim, studying the photographs, had hardly heard her. "Tim, did you hear me?" she said impatiently, sitting beside him. Then she saw what he was looking at.

"That's Helen Murdoch's funeral. She was only twelve when she died. I don't know what she died of."

Beth leaned over Tim to get a better look.

"Is that your ghost, Beth?" Tim said quietly, feeling her tighten up as she studied the photographs.

"Yes," Beth answered, "that's what she's like, except... In a horrible sort of way... Oh, Tim, how did you know?"

"Ivy mentioned her. And then I remembered this."

As she turned the pages of the album, gasps of recognition punctuated the silence. "Sometimes she seems happy," she murmured, "and other times..." A lump formed in her throat. Gradually, she became disturbed by the feeling that she had seen these pictures before. They were like an elusive memory, fragments of a story she had once known well. She came to the end of the album. Closing it, she said, "It's her, isn't it? But why is she haunting me?"

In the silence that followed this question, they heard Gran saying goodbye to Mrs Hurst. When she came in, she found them looking unnaturally solemn. "Now, Beth," she said, "you're not starting to worry about this concert already?" With a swift look at his sister, Tim took charge. "It's not the concert, Gran," he said. "We were just looking at this album, and we came across pictures of that girl again, you know, Helen Murdoch. She died suddenly when she was twelve and we were wondering why."

"Ah, that poor mite," said Gran with a sigh. "She didn't really stand a chance. She had some kind of illness and no one seemed to realize how serious it was – except perhaps my great-aunt Minnie. I was reading some-thing about that the other day." She stopped to think. "Yes, Minnie's diary. It's all in that.

Hang on while I find it."

She found and showed them the little grey book. Beth stared in fascination at Minnie's small, ill-formed copperplate handwriting.

"By all accounts," said Gran, "Helen's father was a strict, bad-tempered man. They were all afraid of him, Helen more than anyone, I should think. I'll read you a bit of this. The funeral; let me see…" and she leafed through the book, frowning slightly. Then she began to read aloud.

"That poor Miss Helen! Her father criticizing her piano playing, shouting at her when she gets things wrong. What's he got to complain of, I should like to know, when his own playing is so bad. He drives her too hard; but for what? That's what I can't fathom. No good will come of it. I've tried hinting about this to the Mistress but she only frowns and makes me feel I'm interfering. I wonder Miss Marshall doesn't say something about it…"

Gran sighed and shook her head. She slowly turned a few more pages. She was not aware of how closely Beth was listening, how tightly the girl clenched her hands. "There's a lot more like that," Gran said. "Minnie must have been really worried about that girl. She writes about little else at this time… Yes, listen to this."

"*This morning Miss Helen complained of breathlessness and of pain in her chest. She looked so tired I took it upon myself to forbid her to get up and I went to the Mistress, demanding that a doctor be sent for. I know it's not my place to do so, but if I hadn't… Oh, that poor girl. I couldn't help listening outside her room when the doctor came. I heard him say that the child should have no exertions at all; that she was not even to play the piano. When he said that Miss Helen let up such a wail that the Mistress begged the doctor to allow her at least half an hour a day when she was well enough to get up. That seemed to pacify the girl a little. But then the Master said that it was probably the piano – all the time she spends on it – that was the cause of her weakness. It nearly took my breath away to hear him, of all people, say that. There was such an argument, then, between the two of them, with the child silent, but the Mistress got her way in the end. I've never known her to insist on anything before, never mind raise her voice. Anyway, after they had all gone, I went into see Miss Helen. She was reading a score, something she's written herself, she said. I told her to rest but she shook her head and said something I've been pondering about ever since. 'There's no time,' she said 'There's no time…'"*

Beth leaned back and closed her eyes. She had gone rather white. Gran leafed through a few more pages. "Go on," said Tim. "What happened?"

"The maid told me that the child spends half the night composing some piece of music. The child swore the maid to secrecy. Now what am I to do? If I say anything to the Master or Mistress the child will be in trouble again. I can't bring that on her. I'll have to talk to her myself…" Gran turned the page. *"At one o'clock this morning I found the child sitting up in bed scribbling in that book of hers." I tried to scold her but all she said was that she had to finish the sonata she's writing. It's the best thing she's ever done, she said, and she implored me not to say anything. I was just about to get angry with her when she started coughing. That really*

*shook me. It's not an ordinary cough. I hope that
doctor knows what he's doing…"*

Suddenly, Beth herself doubled up in a fit of coughing. It was so violent and unexpected, Gran rushed across to her and held her in her arms until the coughing subsided. She sent Tim hurrying for a glass of water. Beth quickly recovered. "I don't know what happened," she said. "I was thinking so hard about Helen; and then I had this terrific itch in my throat." She sipped the water thankfully.

Gran tucked the diary away in her bureau. She had forgotten how impressionable Beth could be.

On the way home, Tim said, "I'm going to *Whit's End* tomorrow to see Ivy. They'll want to know whether you're going back there for another lesson. After last time…"

Beth hung her head. She kicked a stone along the gutter. "I don't know," she said finally. "I've really missed the lessons. And I need Megan's help to practise for the concert, but…"

"I'll be there," Tim offered. "And if it's only the ghost of a girl you're afraid of…" Beth looked at him in disbelief. Even now he did not seem to understand.

Tim returned from *Whit's End* the next day and said to Beth, "Megan said you're not to return until you feel happy to do so. She said she was sorry if anything upset you – I could hardly say what upset you, though – but you're not to worry. And she was really excited about the concert, you should have seen her. She wants you back, Beth, I'm sure."

What he didn't tell her about was his sudden, irrational dislike of Megan. They had spoken briefly in the music-room, but a mutual suspicion had sprung up between them, keeping the conversation short, stilted, polite. "She gives me the creeps," Tim said to himself. "She's so different from Ivy."

Beth's fears slowly subsided. One morning, she woke with the certainty that she must go back to the house, ghost or no ghost. She needed – she ached for – the lessons; without them she felt restless and bored. After all, what harm could the ghost really do her?

Chapter 10
Helen's Manuscript Book

That same evening Beth sat at her desk flicking through scores. Her head buzzed with ideas for the concert programme. She wanted to draw up a short-list of pieces she might play to present to Megan the next day. Two hours later she had a list that almost reached the foot of the page. She looked at it with despair. However was she going to decide?

She heard Tim go to bed. Then her mother came in to find out what she had been doing. Beth showed her the list and chatted about the concert.

"Is that why you're going back to Megan?" her mother asked.

"I want the lessons, Mum," said Beth. "Especially as I'm going to do a new programme at the concert. She doesn't work me *that* hard." It was an echo of an earlier conversation, and her mother knew better than to persist with it. She said good night.

Beth felt too keyed up to go to bed. Apprehensively, she drew out her score pad and opened it. Was this the sonata Helen was working on just before she died? Beth was aware of the strangeness of the question even as it formed in her head. And she knew the answer.

An idea came to her. It was so unexpected, so exciting, her heart seemed to lurch. Why not play the unfinished piece at the concert? She had the whole of the first movement. What a wonderful idea! She hummed the piece to herself.

The room grew colder. She stiffened; her heart thumped in panic. There was *something* in the room. She was about to scream when she felt her whole body freeze into immobility. A darkness closed over her mind and she felt a coldness invade every part of her. She was no longer in control… Picking up her pen, she turned to a clean page in her pad, and began to write the first notes of the sonata's second movement. Her pen flowed unceasingly across the page.

But about half way through the second movement, the regular flow of the pen began to slow down. There were pauses and crossings out. The notes became spidery and tentative. Suddenly the pen jerked about crazily in her grasp; then it shot from her hand as if an unseen force had plucked it from her. Simultaneously, a pain which had been building up in her chest became acute. She staggered up, feeling like a swimmer striking frantically upwards for air after breaking free of a deadly entanglement.

And then her body calmed itself, her eyes became heavy, her mind became blank. Once more she picked up the pen and began to write.

In the morning, she shoved the score into her desk. It gave her the shivers even to look at it.

* * *

For days she debated with herself: should she return to *Whit's End*? Twice she had seen the ghost there... She was scared. But she loved the lessons; Megan seemed to anticipate everything she wanted to know, things she could never have worked out for herself, and she knew she was making rapid progress. That *mustn't* stop. She *had* to go back. Ghost or no ghost.

On the way to *Whit's End*, Beth rehearsed what she was going to say to Megan to explain the extraordinary exit she had made on her last visit. But when Megan opened the door and welcomed her, she felt the words melt away, leaving only a sense of shame and embarrassment. "Megan, I'm really sorry," she tried to begin.

"Don't worry about it, Beth," Megan interrupted. She seemed nervous herself: her hand fluttered, her voice had a catch in it. "We won't talk about it. I think that's the best thing, don't you?" That surprised Beth. It did not seem right to have her terror brushed aside like this. She tried again. "It was horrible... I saw..." But she could not put it into words, especially with Megan watching her so apprehensively.

Megan led her into the music-room. "Look," she said. "Whether you saw anything or not is beside the point." Beth stiffened. "What I mean is, this house affects people in odd ways. It has an atmosphere which some people are very sensitive to. It might be haunted…" Here she paused and bent her head, as if regretting these last few words. "But you mustn't let it play on your imagination. Now, promise me you will put it completely out of your mind."

Beth stared at her in dismay and puzzlement. She was relieved that Megan had made it all so easy for her. But did the woman believe, then, that she had made it all up, acted like some hysterical, highly-strung girl? She was about to protest when Megan abruptly arose and went to the piano. She began to play. With a sigh, Beth joined her.

They played pieces that Beth had practised before. Megan seemed to be holding back her criticism, as if afraid to say anything that might upset the girl.

At eleven Ivy brought in some coffee. Putting down the tray, she said determinedly, "Megan, I think Beth's probably done enough for one morning, don't you?" Megan frowned. "No, enough," Ivy said firmly. "Beth, come and sit beside me. I want to hear more about this concert that Tim has been telling us about."

She sat beside Ivy and told the sisters about Mrs Hurst and the concert.

Megan said, "And have you decided yet what you're going to play?" There was a peculiar eagerness in her question that made Ivy look at her suspiciously. Beth smiled. She drew from her pocket the list she had drawn up the previous night and handed it to Megan. "I'd like to play lots of things," she said. "But I can't decide." Megan ran her eyes slowly down the list, nodding. Then she looked searchingly at Beth.

Beth flushed. "She's guessed," she thought.

Megan said, "There's something I'd like to add to your list, Beth. Something quite special," and she hurried from the room without explanation.

Ivy looked after her thoughtfully. She turned to Beth. "I think I know what Megan's gone to fetch," she said, shaking her head. "It's a piece written by a relative of ours, oh, many years ago. Megan's a bit obsessed with it. She always gives it to her pupils to play at some time or other. It's very precious to her." Then she added, as if to herself, "But I wish she wouldn't."

There was an embarrassed silence. Beth did not know what to say.

"Come on," said Ivy, getting up. "I think it's time you were on your way." They went out into the hall.

Megan hurried down the stairs carrying a large, brown book. She held this out to Beth and said, "This is Helen's music book. She wrote all her compositions in this. It's the most valuable thing that I possess, Beth, but I'm going to trust you with it for a while. I want you to have a look at the last piece in the book. It's unfinished and — and I know it won't be entirely new to you, but... Well, see what you think."

Beth took the book. As she felt its weight, and studied the pattern embossed in the cover, she felt a shiver of excitement. She ran her hands over it and held it close as she said goodbye.

She did not open the music book until she got home. The early pages were covered with neat, childish notation; there were little scribbles in the margin, too. As she turned the pages, she noticed how the notation became more fluent, more and more like the notes she had been writing so mysteriously herself. Here was proof if ever she needed it.

She shivered. Proof of what?

She turned back to the flyleaf. Neat hand-writing said, "This book belongs to Helen Florence Murdoch. Her Composition Book. Volume One. 1908–19…" An indescribable feeling of sadness, of a haunted memory, came over her as she read those words.

Remembering what Megan had said, she turned to the last piece in the book. *Sonata in Cm*. This score was already familiar. She propped it on the piano and began to play.

The first movement flowed with almost no faltering. But as she played, that familiar feeling of dread crept up on her. It became more powerful at the start of the second movement. Then, once more, came the pain, the breathlessness, the sensation of choking, and she had to stop. She turned the pages, thinking, why is this happening? until she came to the last page of the score. Here, there was a little, waving trail of ink ending in a large blot. She imagined Helen clutching her throat, falling, blood trickling from her mouth. Suddenly, she felt pity for the girl.

She carried the book upstairs. There, she compared the score in the book with the one on her pad. Identical, even down to the blot. But the new score carried on from there.

Now, at last, Beth began to understand.

Chapter 11
Nightmares

The following afternoon Beth went for a walk. She eventually made her way into the leafy quietness of the wood and wandered under the trees where it was cool and shadowy. At one point she paused, then remembered that it was here, at this very spot, that she had first spoken to Megan. Was it only three weeks ago? She recalled the silhouette moving through the sunlit trees towards her; and she asked herself again: how much did Megan really know about the ghost?

She sat on a log to rest. It was a warm day with little breeze. She closed her eyes and tried to empty her mind. Gradually, she relaxed.

There was a faint noise, like a curl of breeze in some leaves. Shielding her eyes from the glare, she thought she saw a girl's face between the leaves not far away. It was only for a second, but Beth knew that face. She jumped up and took a few steps forward. She saw, unmistakably, the girl's dress flit through the shrubbery. Beth felt such a spurt of excitement and fear that she had to hold on to a tree to steady herself.

Further up the path she saw the girl again, all of her this time, red hair falling to her shoulders, her dress passing through brambles as if it had no substance. Beth hurried after her. She wanted to call out to her but her voice could not get past the tightness in her throat. The girl did not look around; she turned a corner and disappeared from view. When Beth reached the same spot, the girl was nowhere to be seen. Beth hurried on, feeling a sudden despair: had she lost her? She came to a small gate barely visible beneath over-hanging trees. Peering into the garden beyond it, she recognized with surprise where she had been led. It was the hidden garden at the bottom of *Whit's End*. She hadn't realized that it could be reached through the woods.

"Hello?" Beth called nervously. There was no answer and she felt foolish. She opened the gate and stole into the garden, making her way slowly to the summerhouse. There she sat and waited, starting at every faint noise and unexplained whisper.

Drowsiness overcame her. She closed her eyes.

And there was Helen shimmering in front of her. The ghost's face was a ghastly white, her eyes dark smudges, her dress like layers of mist. The hair had turned from waves of red to a stiff, wiry grey as if covered in frost. Her mouth opened and closed silently like lips under water. Beth was too frightened to make sense of that silent speech. She felt herself floating adrift of all that she knew. And then she was being drawn out of herself like a thin thread; she was being drawn into the black void of the ghost's eyes. There pictures formed: of the score, of a keyboard, of a church with an audience, of a girl playing. She heard the faint music and she fastened on to that. The music grew louder; and as it did so it drew her back into the air, back inside herself, to what she knew. And the ghost began to fade.

When the music stopped, Beth lost consciousness.

Tim and Ivy had spent the afternoon on the section of his project concerned with the house's garden. As the old photographs showed, it had once been magnificent, especially during his great-great-uncle Harry's time, as Ivy pointed out. They arranged the sequence of photographs, which Ivy said she would get copied, and they thought up captions for each.

The work had made Tim curious to see the garden again, so Ivy let him out the back way, through the half-ruined conservatory. He wandered around, noting the changes he had documented, and came eventually to the little summerhouse. From a distance, Beth's slumped form resembled a heap of discarded clothes, but on realizing that it was his own sister lying there, he crept up to her, thinking to surprise her. Her face was white, there was no sign of life. Tim stared at her, puzzled. He shook her, felt her coldness, cried out, "Beth, Beth, wake up." She was limp when he tried to lift her, but she moaned softly, to his great relief. He held her on his lap and gently slapped her face. Her eyes opened and he lifted her on to the seat. She held her head, wincing with pain. "Beth, what happened? Are you ill?"

"Tim," she said faintly, "what are you doing here?"

"What happened? Did you faint?"

"I don't know. I..." Then she seemed to remember.

"You look ghastly. What's the matter?"

"I saw her again."

"Who? You mean...?"

Beth nodded. "She looked horrible. She was trying to speak to me, I think. Then there were pictures, and I was floating in blackness..."

"Come on, Beth," Tim ordered. "I'm going

to get you home." Unsteadily, she got to her feet and Tim helped her to walk down the summerhouse steps.

But as they came out on to the lawn, they encountered Megan. She appeared to be waiting for them. They stared at each other. Beth looked at her feet. Tim frowned: he had never felt comfortable with Megan and in this moment all his vague misgivings about her crystallized into hostility.

"I thought I heard voices," Megan began. It made them sound like trespassers.

"My sister's just had a terrible fright," Tim shouted accusingly. "Leave her alone."

Megan stepped anxiously towards Beth. "What happened?" she asked, grasping Beth's arm and searching her face. "You look dreadful."

Beth shook her head.

Tim butted in. "You know what she saw," he shouted again. He knew he was losing control of himself; but something told him Megan was at the root of his sister's troubles. "Why can't you leave her alone?"

Megan glared at him in surprise and

contempt. She turned away from him and tried to draw Beth to her. "What's the matter, Beth? What did you see?"

"Her," Beth muttered.

"Who?"

Beth just looked at her, and Megan, understanding, took a step back.

"She wants me to do something," Beth wailed, "but I don't know what it is…"

Tim grabbed her other arm. "Come on, Beth. Let's get out of here."

They moved off, leaving Megan standing in the unkempt grass, gazing after them. When he reached the house, Tim turned and shouted at Megan, "Leave her alone, will you? She was all right until she came here."

Megan scowled, folded her arms, turned and walked away, heading for the wood. Her jerky rhythm betrayed the anger she felt at being talked to in such a way and of the effort it cost her to suppress a retort.

Ivy, meanwhile, attracted by the noise, came around the side of the house. "Beth," she exclaimed. "Are you ill? What on earth's the matter, child?"

"She collapsed in the garden," Tim said. "I think she just blacked out."

"My goodness," said Ivy, alarmed. "I'll take her home. Come on."

In the Land Rover, Beth sat between them, holding on to the seat. Ivy said, "Perhaps you've been overdoing the lessons with Megan. Why not give them a rest?" Beth nodded; she did not feel like talking.

When they arrived home, their mother was out. Beth went straight to bed. Tim thanked Ivy and promised that he would ring Gran if Beth took a turn for the worse.

As Beth dressed the following morning, she felt a weight of sadness inside her. She supposed it was caused by the decision she had come to in the night to stay away from *Whit's End* for the time being – and that meant away from Megan. For she could not imagine Megan coming to her own house to give her lessons; she knew that that was not part of the deal; besides, it wouldn't work, the piano was wrong, the atmosphere...

She found her mum in the dining-room

typing invoices. "Beth, a word," she said, looking at her daughter anxiously. Beth sat at the table, sensing what was to come. "Ivy Browne rang last night, asking how you were. I must say, I did feel rather silly, not knowing what she was talking about. Now you're feeling a bit better, you can tell me what happened."

"I just fainted, Mum, that's all."

Mrs Brooke shook her head sceptically. "Ivy gave me the impression that it's a bit more than that. She thinks you're overdoing the piano lessons. Is Megan expecting too much of you?"

Slowly, Beth nodded. She bent her head to conceal a rush of emotion and a sense of shame at her lie. Her mother regarded her closely, and then she added, "Ivy also said that the thought of the concert is playing on your nerves, that you're more worried about it than you're letting on. Is she right, Beth? Come on, you can tell me. There's no shame in it."

To her dismay, Beth felt tears pricking her eyes. "Not really, Mum," she protested, raising her head. But when her mother got up and slid an arm around her shoulder, Beth sobbed. Her mother tried to comfort her.

When Beth had calmed a little, Mrs Brooke said, "I think you'd better give everything a rest for a bit, don't you? There's no point in letting yourself get into such a state." Beth nodded; she wiped her eyes. "I'll ring Megan and tell her," Mrs Brooke continued. "I think I should have a word with her anyway. And Mrs Hurst too, though I suppose she'll be very disappointed."

"Not Mrs Hurst," Beth blurted out. "Not yet. Let's see."

"Are you sure?" Mrs Brooke said, searching her daughter's face. Beth nodded, feeling a little brighter now.

They talked for a while longer. Then Mrs Brooke said, "I've got a lunch booking today, I'm afraid, but I'll ring Gran and ask if you can spend the day with her. Tim's gone off somewhere; he didn't say when he would be back." Beth protested that she would be all right but her mother said with determination, "I'm not letting you be on your own today,

Beth, not the state you're in. Gran'll be only too pleased to have you."

Walking to Gran's cottage, Beth wondered whether she should tell Gran about the ghost. Gran might understand; it would be a relief to have her as well as Tim on her side. But she imagined Gran's reaction: the doubt first, the questioning, the horror, the anger at Megan; Mum would be drawn in too ... and the piano lessons would *really* end. She became confused. As she knocked on Gran's door, she thought, It's no good, I can't tell her, not until I've really made up my mind about Megan and *Whit's End*.

But she told Gran of her decision to stop the lessons for a while, to give herself a rest. Gran seemed relieved rather than curious. "It's for the best, Beth," she observed. She took Beth into town. They had a meal, wandered around department stores and ended up in a second-hand bookshop where they bought some books.

A sense of emptiness and sadness persisted in Beth all day. She had been shaken by the bout of sobbing in front of her mother – when was the last time that had happened? She had been a little frightened by the way it had risen from some unsuspected depth in her being. She sensed, too – and perhaps this feeling was barely acknowledged – that Helen was watching her, judging her, determined to bend her to her will.

A couple of nights later she had a disturbing dream. In it, Helen was sitting on a gravestone in the local churchyard, humming to herself. She looked young and fresh; her hair stirred in the moonlight. But then a cold wind swept through the yew trees. She slid off the gravestone, skipped through the long grass around the church, and suddenly dropped to her knees by a mound of earth and a newly-planted headstone. With her finger, she traced her name and dates carved into the stone. She turned and looked straight at Beth. Her face was now full of anger. With slow, deliberate movements, she beckoned to Beth, and Beth felt herself being drawn to her. As she approached, the mound of earth caved in and a great, dark pit yawned at her feet. Helen was behind her. She felt a violent push. She was falling and falling...

Beth woke, sweating and terrified.

She had to get up and walk about. It was past three o'clock.

For the rest of the night she was alone with her nightmare.

After lunch the following day, she decided to visit Gran again. But when she arrived at the cottage, she remembered that Gran was working at the baker's. She wondered what to do with herself. She rather dreaded going to the wood now, in case she ran into Megan there. She stood irresolutely in the street. How empty my life is now, she thought; without the lessons there is nothing to do — nothing *worth* doing, that is. The church clock struck two; this gave her an idea. She would see if Helen really did have a grave like the one she had seen in the nightmare.

It was in the shadow of an old yew. For a while she was unable to go near it, it was too similar to the one she had seen in her dream... It was old and roughened now; the inscription on the mottled stone had faded. Beth edged forward and cautiously crouched by the grave. She brushed away the long grass and traced her fingers over the words. *In loving memory of Helen Florence Murdoch, dearly beloved and only daughter... Rest in peace...* Beneath this grave lay the bones of... But the thought frightened her. A few bedraggled flowers hung from a little urn; she wondered if it was Megan who had put them there. Suddenly, she felt an acute sense of sorrow for Helen, caught up in a disease that had killed at the start of her life's work. I'll try and help you, Beth found herself whispering; but she hardly knew what she meant by that.

She left the grave and walked to the front of the church, feeling faintly sick and rather weak. The church door was open. She wandered into its shady coolness and stopped at the central aisle. In the left transept was the piano. The sight of it made her feel hungry for its sound, for the feel of the keys. She sat on the piano stool and opened the piano lid. The tone of the instrument pleased her. In the stool she found some scores. She began to play. Her tension, anxiety, fear flowed into the music. It was exhilarating. The sound filled the church.

Mrs Hurst came in. She was carrying a large bunch of flowers from her garden. She stood nearby in the shadows and listened. She understood then why a journalist had used the word "prodigy", even if it had been an exaggeration.

When Beth rounded off a piece and reached up for another score, Mrs Hurst came into view. Beth started guiltily, then smiled.

"Are you practising for the concert, Beth?"

Was that what she was doing? Having tried the piano, she felt she *could* go through with the concert; it all depended on what she chose to play.

But as she did not immediately answer, Mrs Hurst looked concerned. "Is there a problem?" she asked.

Beth shook her head. "Oh, no, I hope not. Mum's just a bit worried that I've been overdoing it, you see, what with the lessons and…"

Mrs Hurst examined the girl's pale, strained face, the touch of sadness in her eyes. "Well," she said, putting down the flowers on the piano, "if you would like me to talk to your mother about it…"

"No, I'll be all right." She smiled re-assuringly. "Did you hear me playing? Do you think I'm good enough?"

"Good enough?" laughed Mrs Hurst. "You'll put the other musicians to shame, I fear. You go on playing like that, Beth, and you've got a great future ahead of you."

Beth knew she was exaggerating; why do so many people do that, she wondered. But she was grateful for Mrs Hurst's comments. She asked, "Would you like to hear some more?" As she played, she said to herself, I don't have to play Helen's unfinished sonata, she can't make me. I can do the same programme as I did at school.

The thought should have comforted her, but it didn't.

The second of Beth's two nightmares was even worse than the first. Helen, as if feeling betrayed and angry, was no longer the fresh young girl skipping towards the grave. She was white and cold and fierce. They were in the music-room at *Whit's End*. Beth was at the piano. Helen was behind her with an icy hand on her shoulder. Beth was composing the fatal second movement of the sonata. Approaching the point where the music broke off, she struggled vainly to free herself from Helen's grip. The pressure in her head increased, the pain in her chest was reaching bursting point. The pen she picked up to write on the staves seemed enormously big. She pressed down, the nib snapped, there was black ink everywhere. She was wading through it, sinking into it, coughing and coughing.

"Wake up, Beth, wake up." Tim was shaking her, looking scared. He stood there in his pyjamas, and watched her struggle to come to her senses. "You were making the most ghastly noise," he said. She looked awful, her face was pinched and white, sweat glistened on her cheeks.

She sat up, blinking in the glaring light. Finally, she said, "It's Helen. She won't leave me alone. It's as if she wants me to go through what she went through."

"It was only a nightmare, Beth."

Beth shook her head. "She's inside me. *Inside me*. I can't get rid of her." They stared at each other. Tim felt helpless. Beth hid her face in her hands and said, fatally, "I've got to do what she wants. She won't leave me alone if I don't."

"What does she want?"

"To finish that sonata she was composing when she died. That's why she's still here, haunting me; she won't let go until it's finished, until…"

"Well?"

"Until I play it in the church, just as she was going to." Beth's face cleared; she had finally put it into words. How simple it sounded.

"So what's the problem?" Tim asked.

Beth looked at him in despair. "She died while she was composing that second movement, remember? And every time I get near to playing that part, I feel as if I'm dying too. That's what I was dreaming of just now."

Tim shook his head, baffled. "But you can't die like that, Beth," he protested, alarmed at this dangerous talk. "It's silly."

Beth turned on him. "How do you know?" she hissed, her face contorted. "Helen died, didn't she? I might die too."

Beth was quiet and brooding all the next day. Tim stayed around, and she was grateful for that.

He was now becoming seriously concerned. How much of this should he keep to himself? How much should he try and tell Mum or Gran?

When Mrs Brooke came home and was unpacking dishes in the kitchen, Tim tried to break into her patter about the lunch booking, but he found no opening. The longer he left it, the more impossible it seemed to become. And then she flared up at him when she found he had failed, contrary to a promise that morning, to cut the grass, and he got the by now familiar lecture on pulling his weight, etc., around the house. She was in no mood to hear about ghosts.

He thought about telling Gran, but the more he went over the story in his mind the more fantastic it became. She would be worried, too, there would be a row, and Beth might not forgive him. It was all so complicated. He decided to bide his time, reflecting that as the visits to *Whit's End* had stopped, the problem might solve itself. Except…

That night Beth, in a trance, wrote out the third movement of the sonata.

Chapter 12
Collapse

A few days later Tim came down from his room looking rather self-satisfied, clutching a big folder. He said to Beth, who was sitting at the piano, "I've finished my project at last. I'm going to take it up to show Ivy." She looked up with interest. "Do you want to come with me?" he added, tentatively. Then he remembered their last visit, Beth's blackout and the loss of his temper with Megan. "Oh, but I suppose not," and he turned to go.

The prospect, however, filled Beth with a sudden longing. She had come to the conclusion that Megan might be keeping things back from her, but she did not have to fear her. And then there was the transcript of the sonata's third movement, the one she had scored in the night – she had to show Megan that, it was just too good, too strange, too amazing to keep to herself. She felt she had to talk to Megan too, about what was going on; for the more she thought about it, the more she saw that Megan alone held the key to Helen's real intentions. "I said I'd return Helen's music book," she said. "But I don't know whether I should go up there. I promised Mum and Gran…"

"I'll take it, then."

Beth shook her head. "No, I ought to go myself. I owe that much to Megan. One more visit won't hurt. You won't tell Mum, will you?"

But Tim wasn't having that. "Mum's got to know," he said decisively.

"She's not here."

"Then leave her a note."

Beth smiled at him. Sometimes his cleverness surprised her. She scribbled on a piece of paper, "We've both gone to *Whit's End*. Don't worry."

* * *

Megan greeted Beth nervously. For the first few minutes they were both tongue-tied. Beth mumbled apologies and tried to explain that she had not been well. "So I understand," said Megan, coldly. There was an awkward pause. Megan pointed to Helen's music book. "Did you find it interesting?"

"Oh, yes," Beth said, relieved. "Especially the last one..."

"The unfinished sonata."

Beth took a deep breath; her heart began to beat faster. "Megan," she began, "you remember on one of my first visits I wrote out some music – some music I thought I was hearing – but that it wasn't written in my handwriting?"

"Of course," said Megan, suddenly alert. "But you shouldn't let that worry you."

Beth interrupted. "No, I must talk about it, Megan." She flipped open Helen's book. "See? The handwriting is exactly the same."

Megan glanced at the score. She gave the girl a piercing look. She asked quietly, sharply, her head slightly to one side, "What are you trying to say, Beth?"

Beth felt herself trembling inside. Why was Megan making it so hard for her? She was at a loss to know what to say next. Then she had a thought. She pulled her own score pad from beneath Helen's book and opened it. "That's what I wrote a few nights ago," she said.

Megan took the book. She stared at the score, then she stiffened in excitement. She flicked back through the pages to the beginning of the second movement, then moved forward, pausing here and there to hum a phrase, making little exclamations, her fingers moving at times on the page as if she was feeling for the notes. Coming to the point in the second movement where the original score had broken off, she stared at the ink blot. Beth watched her close her eyes and saw a faint tremor pass through her; then she continued reading. At length, she said, "And you wrote all this yourself, Beth?"

Beth whispered, "Not me, Megan. You know that. It was Helen."

Megan's hands began to tremble. She dropped her gaze. "Helen?" she echoed.

"You know what I mean. Surely you do.

Isn't it time we talked about it? I need to. I want to know what's going on."

Megan caught the note of desperation in her voice. "All right," she said, coming to a decision. "Tell me what has been happening. From the beginning."

The story flowed out. The spectral music. The glimpse of Helen in the shrubbery, the clapping on the lawn, the encounters in the wood and the garden. The possessions at night. The transcriptions there on her desk in the morning. The nightmares. The horror of it all. And the pity.

Megan's face had a haunted, sorrowful look. She seemed sorry for the girl, but she offered no comfort. Instead, she said, "All this has a purpose, Beth, believe me."

Beth had been momentarily exhausted by the telling of her tale; and Megan's response was so unexpected, for a while she sat in silence, staring at her hands. "For what purpose?" she was eventually about to ask, but by this time Megan had gone over to the piano with the score of the sonata. "Why don't you come and play this, Beth? That's what all your suffering is about, you know. Come on, it'll cheer us both up."

Beth looked at her in dismay. After all that she had said, was this all that Megan could think of? Bemused, she got up unsteadily, thinking that instead of "having it out" with Megan, the woman had given nothing away. Beth sat at the piano and looked at the score. "Play it from the very beginning," said Megan, a gleam of excitement in her eye.

The sound of the sonata drifted into the room where Ivy was looking through Tim's folder. Hearing it, she paused, cocked her head to one side to hear it better, and muttered, "Not again."

Tim looked at her in surprise. "Don't you like it?"

"No, I don't," said Ivy with some vehemence. She got up. "Wait here, Tim. I've got something I must say to my sister."

Tim watched her march across the hall and fling open the music-room door. "Megan," he heard her shout above the music, "Can I have a word with you." He heard Megan begin to protest; but Ivy was in a formidable mood. "Now, if you please. It can't wait." Megan came out, her face dark. The sisters disappeared into the front-room, closing the door.

Tim sat in the silence for a minute, wondering what was going on. Then he heard Beth begin to play again. He recognized the piece: it was the beginning of what she called Helen's sonata. The ghost's sonata. What a strange thought; could there really be such a thing? He wished he could make up his mind. He went to the door of the music-room. Beth was too absorbed in what she was playing to notice him.

He stood by the window in the hall near the front-room door. He could hear the sisters arguing. What was the problem now? He strained to hear what they were saying but Beth's music drowned out their muffled words.

Then he caught sight of someone coming up the drive. He was astonished to see that it was Gran. She walked with a determined tread and a closed look on her face. Tim knew that look; it meant trouble. He opened the door. "Gran, what are you doing here?"

"Where are they?" said Gran stiffly, stepping into the hall.

Tim closed the door. "In there," he whispered, indicating the front room. "They're having some sort of argument."

Gran looked surprised. "What about?"

"I don't know. I think it must be something to do with what Beth is playing."

"Is that Beth playing now?"

Tim nodded. "Gran," he said, "what are you doing here? And how did you know we were here this morning?"

"I called in and saw Beth's note. And I shouldn't think I need to tell you why I'm here. After what you told me the other day, I'm amazed you let Beth come here again. What were you thinking of?"

Tim blushed slightly and mumbled, "It was to be her last visit, just to return the music book and to say thank you. I didn't think she was going to play."

Beth came to the end of the first movement. In the silence the two in the hall heard Ivy say,

"It mustn't happen again, Megan. You must see that. It's too dangerous. Do you hear me?"

Beth began the second movement.

The door opened and Megan appeared, flushed and annoyed. She started and gasped when she saw Gran standing there. "Ivy, we've got a visitor," she managed to say, and she approached Gran uncertainly, with Ivy peering over her shoulder. She half held out her hand but seeing that Gran clung resolutely to her handbag, she let it drop.

"I'm sorry to intrude like this," said Gran, but there was no regret in her voice. "As you may know, I'm Beth and Tim's grandmother."

Ivy bustled forward. She insisted on shaking Gran's hand. "I'm so pleased to meet you at last, Mrs Browne. The boy's talked about you so much. He's a bright one," she added, nodding toward Tim.

Gran remained distant. "I'd like to thank you for helping him with his project," she said with a polite smile. "But I've not come here to talk about Tim."

Ivy glance swiftly at her sister. "Is it about Beth? We know she hasn't been well."

Gran clutched her handbag more firmly. She cleared her throat. "She was perfectly fine until she came here." The words hung in the air between the three women. Gran herself seemed slightly taken aback at her own bluntness. "What I mean," she said, softening her voice a little, "is that Beth is a very highly strung girl. She has a very strong imagination. She easily becomes over-wrought, and that makes her ill."

Ivy tutted sympathetically. Megan tried to say something reassuring but her flush had grown deeper, she seemed very ill at ease. Tim watched her, thinking, Go for it Gran, tell her what you think.

"She told me that she had given up the piano lessons that you were so kindly giving her, Miss Murdoch, because she found the strain of them too much."

"Now don't worry," said Ivy, trying to be reassuring. "My sister and I were just discussing what to do about Beth when you arrived. And we can see she is not quite herself at the moment. In fact, we were under the impression that the lessons had discontinued. Beth's only playing now because she wants to."

"Is that what you're saying?" said Megan quietly. "That you don't want Beth to have any more lessons? It will break the child's heart."

Gran scowled. She took a step back and swept a glance around the gloomy hall. "What I'm saying – and I think I speak for her mother too – is that I don't think Beth should come here again. We've all seen the effect it's had on her."

"What do you mean by that, Mrs Browne?" Ivy asked, drawing herself up.

Gran gave a sceptical laugh. "Do I have to spell it out? All this talk of ghosts, of some dead girl…" But Gran's voice trailed away. She suddenly remembered that it had been herself who had talked of the girl in the old photographs, had read to her from Minnie's diary.

Megan took advantage of her confusion. "I can assure you, Mrs Brooke," she said, keeping her emotion under control, "that Beth has been treated perfectly well here.

She's been given free lessons –" Gran glared at that – "and I've done my best for her. If she has a strong imagination…"

"Oh, she has that," Gran interrupted sarcastically.

There was an awkward pause. Ivy was shaking her head, Megan was trembling slightly, Tim's heart was beating furiously and Gran was searching for the right words to express her indignation.

"She needs the lessons," Megan insisted. "If you take those away from her she'll never forgive you."

Gran bridled. "I don't know what you're up to," she began, angrily, "but let me tell you that whatever it is, I won't have it. I don't want Beth coming here again, do you understand?"

Megan looked panic-stricken. She tried to speak…

But they were never to hear her words. At this point, Beth's playing faltered. It had been flowing without fault or pause, but now it seemed to waver; the tempo became erratic, the volume uneven. The party in the hall listened as if paralysed: there was something deeply disturbing about this. The music began to break down. Then it broke off completely.

They heard a suppressed cry that filled them with alarm. "Beth," Gran cried. She was the first into the music-room. They were all in time to see Beth rise from the piano as if she was staggering under a great weight. She was clutching her throat. She fell heavily at Gran's feet.

The doctor found nothing specifically wrong with her. As a precaution he suggested various tests at the hospital, but Mrs Brooke, in consultation with Gran, decided that what she needed now more than anything was rest and complete calmness. They had their own diagnosis of Beth's troubles and the doctor's opinion simply lent weight to it.

Beth woke the next morning after a heavy and dreamless sleep. Tim brought up her breakfast.

"Did you see her again?" he said.

She shook her head. "No, it wasn't that. It's the second movement of Helen's sonata – just at the point when she broke off, when she died, I feel –" she clutched her throat to illustrate her point – "a horrible itching, then choking here. It feels like I'm going to die. And there's such a pain in my chest."

"But what causes it?"

"It's what she felt," Beth said quietly. "It's what happened to her." She pushed her breakfast tray to one side and slid back down into the bed. Even thinking about it now tired her.

"But if she wants you to play her sonata," said Tim slowly, making a great effort to make sense of the problem, "why is she putting you through the same experience?"

Beth stared at him, thinking hard. "Perhaps she can't help it," she said. "Perhaps I have to go through what she went through – and *survive*."

Later, Gran and Mum sat either side of Beth and made her promise not to have any more piano lessons with Megan, to stay away from

Whit's End and not to think of playing in the concert unless she was really up to it. She looked at their concerned faces and nodded.

But it's not for me to decide, she thought after they had left. That's what they don't understand.

In the darkness of the night, she sat once again at her desk, her eyes shining, her pen moving along the staves. Before the dawn filtered through her curtains, she had finished transcribing the last movement of Helen's sonata. With a long sigh, she laid down her pen.

Warmth crept into her body. She became conscious of sitting at her desk. She turned and saw Helen's face, young and beautiful now, glowing in the dark. The ghost was smiling at her.

Chapter 13
The Dress

In the days that followed the completion of the sonata, Beth became convinced that the ghost would now leave her alone. Hadn't she done all that Helen wanted of her? She felt happier than she had done for weeks; pride too, and excitement, as she copied the sonata into Helen's music book. Megan had sent it with a get-well card in which she had written, "If you finish the sonata, write it in Helen's book. That's what she has always wanted." But despite this change in her mood, she still had a persistent sense that something, some great effort, was still required of her; she knew what it was, but in her present frame of mind she refused to acknowledge it. Mum and Gran noticed that she was happier; they put it down to the cancelling of the lessons and her part in the concert. The girl had simply over-reached herself.

No further reference was made to Megan or *Whit's End*; on that, there was a conspiracy of silence. But she knew there was unfinished business there. She imagined Megan waiting, increasingly fretful, for some sign from her of what she intended to do.

One afternoon, she went back to the church. She settled at the piano and played the pieces which had been such a success at the school concert. Then she sat for a long time in the silence, picturing herself standing before a congregation, about to play for them, and she felt such a longing for it to happen.

Involuntarily, her fingers played the opening bars of Helen's sonata. The notes threatened to crack her fragile composure, the veneer of normality that she had built around herself. She closed the piano.

She wandered around the church and came to a small commemorative plaque, in pink marble, fixed to the wall. It said, "*In memory of our beloved daughter, Helen Florence Murdoch, 1900 – 1912. She abides with angels.*" "It's a lie," Beth said to herself, obscurely offended by the last sentence. She had a fierce sense of pity, then, for this girl that no one seemed to have understood. Underneath the plaque was a large, dark, carved chair, so old Beth thought that if anyone sat in it it would crumble to dust.

She heard the sound of footsteps. Hurrying into the porch, she bumped into Mrs Hurst who was carrying a basket of cleaning things. "Beth," Mrs Hurst exclaimed. "How are you? I must say, all this talk of your illness had quite alarmed me."

"I'm fine now," Beth smiled. "It was nothing serious."

Mrs Hurst shook her head regretfully. "What a pity it happened just before the concert."

Beth swallowed hard. She looked at the woman anxiously. "I'm really sorry about that. I was wondering whether you have found anyone to take my place." She was relieved to see Mrs Hurst shake her head.

"I'm not sure what we're going to do about it," Mrs Hurst said. "It's going to be a rather short concert without you. I suppose we'll find someone else to take your place; but so many people were looking forward to hearing you play."

Beth held her hands tightly behind her back and said, "Have you told everyone that I won't be playing, then?"

Mrs Hurst shook her head again. "Only the committee."

"Then I've an idea. I could play the same pieces as I played at the school concert. I don't need to practise them much. What do you think?"

At first Mrs Hurst was dubious, but she soon warmed to the idea.

"Mum and Gran might agree if you came and talked to them," Beth added hopefully.

Two days later there was a family conference. With Mrs Hurst's help, Beth was able to convince her mother and Gran that a repetition of her school concert programme would put no strain on her health. "After all," said Gran, "it's got nothing to do with Miss Murdoch, and I'm sure she's the one that's caused the problems, her and that house."

After Mrs Hurst had left, Beth ran up to her room and opened Helen's music book. She hummed her way through it, skipping only the page with the ink blot – that she still could not face. Why am I doing this now? she asked herself. But she knew the answer; to put it into words would be to admit that she was about to deceive them all. All except Megan.

She suddenly took off after lunch, shouting to her mother that she was going for a walk in the woods. Tim, who was cleaning his bike at the side of the house, was struck by the false note he detected in her voice. It made him curious. Her behaviour had rather puzzled him of late. With the sonata finished, and with no more visits to *Whit's End*, Beth seemed to have wiped Helen's ghost from her mind. When he had tried to talk about her, she had clammed up; that had made him suspicious.

He followed her into the wood. She walked rapidly along the path, as if she had a destination in mind. He came to a gate overhung with leaves. Beth was nowhere to be seen. Leaning on the gate, he listened. He heard a voice, faint and intermittent, come from the garden. Climbing over the gate, he was surprised to find himself at the bottom of *Whit's End*. The last time he had been here, he reflected, he had found Beth unconscious in the summerhouse. Why had she come back here, especially when she had promised not to? He crouched and peered through the leaves. There she was, sitting in the summer-house, hands folded on her lap, her eyes closed. She was talking softly, but only, it appeared, to herself. He crept closer to hear what she was saying.

"...You look so different now. I'm not really afraid of you when you are like this. Sometimes you really frighten me... Were you very ill?... Didn't they know?... Why didn't your mother do anything, then?... You must have been terrified of him. I've seen him in some old photographs... My dad's so different – not that I ever see him now..." Beth sighed; there was a long pause. Then she began again. "I wish I could touch you… No, don't come closer, I'll freeze… I know I've got to play it… You needn't get nasty with me again… But I'm really afraid. I feel just what you felt when you died… I don't want to die… I won't, will I?…" She paused again; sighed heavily. "Oh, but it's weird talking to you, I can see right through you… Where do you go, I mean, when you're not here…? How can you not know? Is it like sleeping…?"

Tim shivered; this creepy half-conversation made him feel strange. Was his sister going mad? He wondered what he should do. Should he go up to her and shake her out of it? But she seemed to have fallen asleep. She was now full-length on the seat with her eyes closed. Tim felt a little ashamed, then, of spying on her, but he said to himself, No, she agreed not to come here, she broke her promise. And she still believes in that ghost. He stepped out of hiding. Yet, as he watched her, he hadn't the heart to disturb her. For once, she looked so peaceful. He slipped away, climbed over the gate and set off along the path. As he walked, he decided that for the time being he would say nothing of what he had just seen, but he would let her know that she wasn't going to deceive him, even if everyone else had been taken in.

Beth was dreaming. She was floating down the aisle of the church in Helen's long white dress, a blue sash around her waist, pearls around her neck. The church was full of people clapping, but when she paused to bow, she knew none of them except Megan. The men wore dark suits with gold chains looped across their waistcoats. The women were swathed in elaborate dresses, their hats and bonnets tied with ribbons. Beth had a brief sense of herself floating upwards, out of her body: she was looking down at them all from among the carved wooden angels of the rafters, even looking down at herself taking her bow. It was an extraordinary feeling of lightness, of drifting in space. Then she was back on the ground, in her own body. She was opening Helen's music book on the piano. She was playing...

"Beth? Beth..." Her name came faintly

down the aisle. Megan was rising out of the body of the congregation, calling to her. The call grew louder. "Beth…" Then she felt a hand on her shoulder. Light replaced the shadows of the church. She was awake, blinking, sitting up in the garden. Megan was leaning over her, looking concerned.

When Beth straightened up, Megan's face cleared. "Beth, this is a surprise. You gave me quite a shock when I saw you here. Did you fall asleep?"

Beth leapt up, suddenly eager to tell her everything that had been happening to her. "I'm sorry, Megan," she began. "I know I'm not really supposed to be here. It's just that…" and she drew closer to the woman to whisper, "I see her here. Helen. I was just talking to her."

Megan's eyes narrowed slightly. She gripped Beth's arms tightly for a minute and her face clenched, as if she was about to burst with some terrible inner force. But she said nothing and the moment passed. Just as swiftly, her face resumed its normal appearance. Beth was silent with wonder.

Slowly, they made their way up to the house. Megan said, "You certainly look much better than you did, Beth. I'm so glad. After all that your mother and grandmother said…"

Beth flashed her a guilty look. "I'm not supposed to be here, I know that," she admitted. "But this isn't a lesson, is it? And Helen doesn't frighten me so much, now that I'm doing what she wants… You won't tell anyone I came, will you?"

Megan nodded, absently. "Of course not," she murmured; her mind was on what Beth had just told her. They reached the conservatory door. Opening it, Megan said, "You look so excited, Beth. Has anything happened?"

"I'll tell you inside."

In the music-room, Beth went to the piano. "Listen to this," she said eagerly. She began to play the final movement of the sonata. She visualized the score unfolding before her as she played. It was a happy, resolved piece, suggesting a breaking free of the spirit. When it was over, Megan could hardly contain herself. She paced up and down the room, talking about it; something youthful came alive in her tired eyes. Suddenly, interrupting herself, she turned to Beth and said, "Won't you play the whole of the sonata now? It's something I've waited to hear all my life."

But Beth shook her head. She had never played it all through, something had always prevented her. And she was still frightened to tackle that second movement. "Helen doesn't want it. Not yet," she explained, wondering why she was so sure of her answer.

Megan leaned against the piano. Her eyes were burning. "Please," she implored.

Beth regretted her stubbornness, but she knew she had to refuse; she shook her head.

"Play it," Megan demanded, her voice hoarse, her eyes wide with astonishment at Beth's reply.

Beth flinched. Megan's face had changed again: it was livid, ugly, possessed. "I can't," she whispered, trembling, and she shrunk back as Megan exploded with impatience.

"You can't?" she echoed in derision. "You can't? My life has been made hell by this unfinished sonata, God knows why. And now, at last, it's finished – and you won't let me hear it? Have you no idea…?" But the force of emotion overcame her and she leaned against a chair with a little groan. Shaking, Beth rose to leave; she was terrified, but Megan raised a hand to stop her, and she froze.

"I've got to play it at the concert," Beth rushed out. "Not now. It's what Helen wants. Please."

Megan straightened up, her face calm again but very pale, her hands shaking. The word "concert" seemed to have checked her. With an effort of self-will, she walked the length of the room to put a safe distance between herself and the girl, and said bitterly, "All right, I understand, I've got to wait a little longer. We both have. Helen still gets her way, she always did. Please sit down again. And I'm sorry, I didn't mean to shout at you."

They both sat down. There was a long, tense silence during which Beth stared at the piano keys, her pulse still racing, and Megan stared out of the window, unseeing. Eventually, the woman recollected where she was and looked anxiously at Beth. She came to a decision.

"You must forgive my little outburst. You will, won't you?" Beth nodded. "And I think it's time we had a real talk about all this, don't you? You once asked me about Helen, about her ghost, her spirit, but I didn't really answer you. I wasn't sure how much you should know. But now... Come and sit by me, child. I want to tell you everything. It's time you knew."

Apprehensively, Beth joined Megan on the chaise-longue. The woman gave her shoulder a little squeeze, but Beth remained stiff, unyielding.

Megan told Beth as much as she knew about Helen's short life. "She must have been an extraordinarily talented girl, but her father was too hard on her, and her mother did not really understand her, and she had this terrible illness in her lungs..."

"I told you that I actually see her, didn't I?" said Beth. "In the garden. And about the transcriptions and the bad dreams...?"

Megan was nodding. "Yes, I know all about them. Remember, I was twelve once, and I had red hair, and I could play the piano almost as well as you can..."

To Beth these words seemed to echo strangely; and then understanding at last flooded like sudden light into her mind. "You, too?" she asked, her eyes widening. Megan gave a slight nod. Beth stared at her, stunned at this revelation. Megan's face had taken on that faintly haunted look that Beth had noticed on their first encounter. "Yes," the woman said, "I've seen her too. In this room, in the garden, in my bedroom. And I've transcribed some of that sonata." Hearing this, Beth felt an extraordinary sense of excitement and relief. But so many questions crowded into her mind: was she afraid? Why didn't she finish the sonata? "Did you keep the music?" she asked eventually.

Megan shook her head, surprised at the question. "No," she said. "I burnt it."

"Burnt it?" Beth echoed, uncomprehending.

Megan explained. "I couldn't go through with it. She terrified me. I became ill, just like you did – just as all the girls did – so my parents sent me away to a sanatorium in Switzerland. I was there for over a year, and when I came back it was too late. I wasn't twelve any more, you see. I threw the score on to the kitchen fire. I didn't want any reminder of it, I wanted to forget it all. But, of course, she wouldn't let me. Years later, she came back to haunt me."

"But if you were too old, why did she come back to haunt you?"

"I may have been too old," Megan continued, "but some of my pupils weren't. At first I didn't understand what was happening – after all, I'm talking about thirty years after all that had happened and I had almost forgotten it. But when my third pupil told me that she had seen a ghost of a girl in the summerhouse, I began to understand. The memories flooded back. Helen was trying to find another girl, to haunt her in the same way that I had been haunted, and I thought, I'm not going to play that game. That's when she made my life a misery. She wouldn't leave me alone, especially at night, nightmares, hauntings, trances... I could well have had a breakdown then, I sometimes think." Megan covered her face and sighed. "I had no choice," she said after a while. "She forced me. I had to find girls of the right age and looks and talent... Then you came along. Oh, Beth, I know I have treated you badly, but I was forced to. Try and understand. You're young, you'll soon get over it, I'm sure."

Beth found all this so extraordinary, for a while she could think of nothing to say, even as her head was buzzing with half-formed questions.

Presently, she described the dream she had had that afternoon, of the concert in the church, of her spirit briefly floating among the wooden angels. Megan seemed intrigued by this. She suddenly got up and said excitedly, as if the thought had just occurred to her, "I've got something to show you, Beth. Come upstairs with me."

Mystified, Beth followed her up the stairs. They came to the attic door. Megan opened it and a chill, musty smell closed around them. They climbed to a dusty room; it was full of boxes, old furniture, unwanted items from generations of Murdochs. Megan lifted out of the top drawer of an old chest-of-drawers a flat cardboard box. "We'll take this to my bedroom," she said.

When she opened the box on the bed, Beth gasped. Inside it was a girl's full-length, white, cotton dress edged with lace and circled by an embroidered white waist-band. She recognized that dress at once. Looking at Megan in amazement, she said, "It can't be the same one? Not Helen's?"

"It is. Here, read this." Megan took from the folds of yellowing tissue that wrapped the dress, a black-edged card on which had been written, "*The dress that Helen wore the day she died, August 31st 1912.*" Beth touched the dress. Here, at last, was a tangible link with the real Helen, the girl who had once lived and dreamt here in this house, hoping for a wonderful future. She saw a few faint, tear-shaped spots on the front of the dress and she realized, with horrible fascination, that these were drops of Helen's blood.

Carefully, Megan lifted the dress from the box. She held it against Beth. "Why don't you put it on," she murmured, her eyes shining strangely. Beth backed away at first and shook her head. "No, that's morbid," she protested, with a look of disgust.

"Put it on," Megan insisted, her face becoming hard. Beth couldn't face another outburst; reluctantly, she took the dress, which smelt slightly musty, and held it against herself, looking at herself in the mirror; curiosity overcame her then, to see what she would look like with the dress on. She wriggled out of her jumper and jeans. Megan helped her into the dress and fastened the buttons. Beth studied herself. She drew in her breath sharply. "I *am* Helen," she said wonderingly. "I really am."

Megan murmured, "Not quite." She lifted a string of pearls from her jewellery box and fixed them around Beth's neck. Then something else occurred to her. "Wait here, Beth," she said, hurrying from the room. Beth heard her climb to the attic again.

The girl stared at herself in the mirror. She felt her flesh begin to tingle. She looked swiftly around the room, wondering if Helen might be watching her.

Megan returned with a long blue sash. "I

think this was Helen's, too," she said. "It's very delicate and a bit faded. But try it on." Beth tied it around her waist, fearful that she might tear the fragile material. "Now you are complete," Megan said. Without taking her eyes off Beth, she took from the drawer of her bedside cabinet the little portrait of Helen. Beth recognized it. "Here," said Megan. "Compare yourself." Beth held the picture up to the mirror so that she could study both images. "We're quite alike," she mused. "And yet so different too. I suppose she herself must have stood in front of this mirror all those years ago, wearing this dress."

"And dreaming of playing her own work in public," Megan added. "She never let go of that dream, did she?"

Beth turned to Megan. "I've an idea," she said experimentally. "For the concert…"

Chapter 14
The Concert

On the morning of the concert, Beth rose early. She sat on her bed and tried to focus on the one problem that still faced her – the only one, she now saw, that was truly threatening her. Over the past couple of weeks she had kept up the pretence that she was to play what everyone – except Megan – was expecting her to play; but she had always known that Helen would only let her play one thing. It wasn't so much the deception that troubled her – although that was bad enough – as the thought of playing the second movement. She realized now that Helen must be powerless to prevent the pain and the choking: it was the one thing that must have defeated her all this time, the one thing that had kept her in limbo.

Presently, she became aware of Tim standing in the doorway, watching her. "Isn't there any privacy in this house," she complained, wondering how long he had been there.

Tim ignored this. "I want a word with you, Beth."

She sensed an edge to his voice. "What about?"

"The concert." He came in, shut the door, and stood looking down on her, frowning.

"What about it?"

"I think I know what you're really going to play tonight."

Beth busied herself straightening the bedclothes. "Do you?"

"You don't fool me, Beth." She sensed his hostility and looked at him in alarm. "All that stuff about playing the school concert pieces isn't true, is it?" Beth stared at him in dismay. "Is it?" he insisted, raising his voice. Reluctantly, Beth shook her head. She felt herself blushing slightly. "You're going to play Helen's sonata, aren't you?"

"I might."

"I thought so."

" So?"

"Oh, you know what I mean. You've told me often enough how it makes you feel. It's dangerous, isn't it? Or don't you believe in all that stuff now?"

"I don't have a choice," Beth protested.

Tim's expression softened. He sat on the bed. "Of course you do," he said. "Don't you?"

She shook her head. It was not so much that she was frightened Helen might become threatening again, haunting her whenever she felt like it, if she did not play the sonata – although that fear was real enough. At a deeper level, she wanted to release the ghost from its torment. As Megan had said, only she could do it. "I can't expect you to under-stand, Tim," she said. "She's relying on me. I have to play it in the church. I *have* to."

"And what if you faint again? In front of everyone?"

Beth looked helpless. "I won't," she said. "I won't." But Tim had put his finger on the problem. "I can't let her down. Besides," she added, "there's also Megan…"

"What about her?"

"She told me that when she was my age Helen haunted her too. She wrote some of the sonata as well, just like I did. But Megan got too ill and was sent away. Now Helen haunts her too, and she won't leave that house until… Megan thinks I may be her last chance."

Beth sounded so reasonable while she was saying this, Tim was surprised to see her cover her face in despair. "And you really believe all that?" he asked.

"I *know* it's true." She studied her brother, trying to guess his intentions. "You won't spoil it all, will you, Tim? You won't tell Mum or Gran?"

Tim got up. "I don't know," he scowled, thoroughly confused. "I'm going to think about it."

On the way to the fête, Mrs Hurst called in with some concert programmes. "Well,

Beth," she smiled, "I'm pleased to see you looking so well. How do you feel? Nervous?"

"A bit," said Beth. "But that's normal, isn't it?"

"So they tell me. But you're ready for tonight? Everything rehearsed?"

Mrs Brooke joined in. "She's practised those pieces to death, I should think. If she's not ready now, she never will be."

Beth took a programme and saw inside it her name and a list of the works she had promised to play. Tim read it aloud over her shoulder. "Chopin, Mendelssohn, Schubert and Scott Joplin. They're certainly getting their money's worth," he added sarcastically.

Mrs Hurst flashed him a puzzled look. "There's a lot of people looking forward to Beth's playing, young man," she said. "You should be proud of your sister."

Tim flushed. "Oh, I am," he said, and biting back his words, he turned and hurried from the room. His mother raised her eyebrows at Mrs Hurst as if to say, "Adolescence," and Mrs Hurst smiled wryly. Beth, however, felt a sharp sense of relief that he had not let on, but how much more provocation would he take? He could ruin everything.

She decided to be as nice to him as she could be. When they got back from the fête, they had a picnic lunch in the garden. Beth took care to offer the sandwiches to Tim first, to fetch him another can of Coke, to give him first choice of the cakes. "He should be running around after you, today," Mrs Brooke complained. Tim grimaced. She interpreted this as, "Don't think you can get round me that easily." But still he did not say anything and Beth began to think that he might not. Or was he just biding his time until Gran came?

After lunch, Tim went back to the fête. Beth mooched about the garden, unable to settle to anything or to lie in the sun like her mother. Eventually, Mrs Brooke insisted on a final run-through of the pieces she was to play that evening. "Go on, Beth. I shall be listening," she said encouragingly. To her mortification, Beth had to play them in the knowledge that she was deceiving her mum with every note. This depressed her. She rattled through the pieces as quickly as she could. When she had finished, she told her mum that she was going for a walk. "Not too far," warned Mrs Brooke, "and nowhere near *Whit's End*. Promise?" Beth nodded.

She walked briskly through the village, up by the tennis courts, past the allotments, along a narrow, shadowy path at the back of the new estate, until she found herself near the church. As she walked, she played the sonata to herself, skirting around that part in the second movement that gave her so much trouble. She sat on a seat near the lych-gate.

Voices came from the open door of the church. She guessed it was being prepared for the concert. She imagined herself inside it that night, just emerging from the vestry to polite applause; and she suddenly realized that she would have to give a little introductory speech to explain the change in the programme and to say something about Helen. The thought of this made her panic. Jumping up, she paced up and down the path, rehearsing what she should say. "Ladies and gentlemen. I want to... I have an announcement to make... The programme

I promised… The pieces I intended to play tonight…" Oh, how would she ever manage it?

The church clock struck four. She hurried home. Gran had just arrived from the fête; she was sitting in the living-room, reading a programme. Mrs Brooke was pouring her a cup of tea. Tim had his head buried in a magazine. Beth gave them all a swift look to see whether Tim had told her secret. She sighed almost audibly when she guessed he hadn't. She noticed he was ignoring her, though.

"Beth," Gran welcomed her. "Just in time for tea. How are you feeling?"

"Fine, Gran," Beth answered, taking a mug from her.

"Now, Beth," Gran continued. "What have you decided to wear tonight? I don't suppose your mother's given a thought to it." Mrs Brooke threw up her hands to her face in mock embarrassment and Gran waved a mocking finger at her. "There, what did I tell you?"

Beth blushed. Luckily, Gran misinterpreted this. "You don't mean to tell me you haven't given it a thought, either? Well, I never." Tim laughed. Beth felt she could have kicked him. "Then I think we'd better go upstairs and see what you've got, young lady."

Beth followed her upstairs. Here was another deception. She had not realized what a strain it could be to deceive them all so deliberately. But as Gran pulled some dresses from the wardrobe, Beth recalled the look of herself in Helen's dress, twirling before the mirror in Megan's bedroom. There was no way that she could wear anything else, but she could hardly tell Gran that.

Eventually, they chose a long blue dress. Gran took it downstairs to iron.

Beth met Tim on the stairs. "Thanks," she whispered. He brushed past her. Pausing at the top of the stairs, he called, "It's not right, Beth. But it's your funeral." He went into his room and slammed the door.

Beth felt she needed more space to think. "Mum, I'm going to have a bath," she called. Lying in the water, she said to herself, Why am I doing this? Why am I deceiving my family? Why does Tim hate what I'm doing?

How can I have the nerve to stand up in front of all those people and tell them that they are going to listen to something quite different to what they expect?

She shivered in her towel. It was not too late. She could still play what was in the programme. Maybe she would make up her mind at the last minute.

Mrs Hurst had saved a pew for the family at the front of the church. Beth wanted to be as inconspicuous as possible, but walking down the aisle in her blue dress, clutching a batch of scores, she felt the eyes of the audience upon her, including several girls from her class at school. When she sat on the pew her legs felt weak and she was as taut as a drumskin inside. Mrs Brooke touched her arm. "Are you OK, Beth?"

Beth nodded. "Just nervous," she replied, attempting a smile.

"You were nervous before the school concert, remember?"

"I know," said Beth, "but it went all right, didn't it?"

"They called you a prodigy, remember?" Tim chimed in, sarcastically. He was sitting on the other side of Gran and he leaned forward to say this. Beth ignored him.

Gran said, "You've got the first half to get in the mood. That should help, shouldn't it?" Beth nodded.

I wish you'd all stop being so nice to me, she thought.

Tim spoke again, in the same sarcastic tone, "Beth, why don't you put those scores under your seat? You won't be needing them, will you." She did as he suggested, throwing him a warning look as she straightened up. Gran noticed this; she whispered with theatrical loudness, "He's just a bit jealous, Beth. Take no notice of him."

Mrs Hurst brought the vicar to them. They all shook hands and made polite conversation.

Where was Megan? Beth turned to look. The church was full. Evening sunlight shone in a band on a section of the audience. She scanned the rows of heads, pretending not to see people she knew who were staring at her. What if something had happened to Megan?

What if she couldn't come? Beth knew she could not play Helen's sonata without Megan there.

Then someone touched her shoulder and called her name. She turned with a start and there was Megan. She was wearing a long black dress trimmed with lace and silk ribbons; there was a silver pendant around her neck. Her hair was tied back, her face heavily made up.

"Oh, Megan, I was just looking for you."

"We're over there," she said, pointing to a row of seats on the left. Beth, looking over, saw Ivy there, watching them; she gave a little wave. "Everything is ready," Megan said quietly.

"Everything?" Beth echoed, wondering what she meant. Megan searched her face with concern. "Oh, you mean…" Beth began, but stopped herself in time. "Yes, everything's ready," she answered with a smile.

"Then I'll see you in the vestry at the interval." Megan nodded slightly to Mrs Brooke and Gran and returned to her seat.

Gran whispered to Beth, "Why does she

want to see you in the interval?"

"Just a last bit of advice, you know, Gran."
Beth straightened up and faced the choir stall
and the altar. Lies are coming easy to me, she
thought.

The clock struck seven. The vicar appeared
in his pulpit and after a few words of thanks
to the organizers and the audience, he intro-
duced the first performer, a boy who was to
play the violin.

He played from memory.

Beth thought, I know I can play the whole
sonata from memory. But what if I forget? Did
I put the score in with the others? She knew
she had, but the mere suggestion that she
might have forgotten it ruined her enjoyment
of the boy's playing. As soon as he had finished
and was taking his bow, she was rummaging
among the scores under her seat. There it was.
What a relief! She held it tightly on her lap.
Calm down, she told herself, calm down.

Now a young woman was sitting before a
magnificent harp and in a confident voice she
was telling the audience about the piece she
was about to play. The notes of the harp were

extraordinarily clear and resonant in the church; Beth was arrested by the sound. The instrument was a revelation, she had never seriously listened to it before. It was only when the applause had died down that she realized that for a while she had forgotten her own role in the concert that night.

A boy singer was now standing before them on steps beneath the rood-screen, in front of a score. He glanced nervously at the audience. Beth could almost feel him beating down his nerves. The organ began to play. She watched him concentrate on the music and saw how that gave him the confidence he needed. His voice soared. Beth looked up at the shadowy roof with its wooden hammer-beams and she could just make out carved wooden angels looking down at them.

Concentrate on the music, she told herself, just as the boy is doing, that's the only way to get through the night. And she did. She pushed everything else from her mind, entered the music as fully as she could, winced at the occasional mistakes and applauded enthusiastically.

Before she knew it, the interval had arrived. Wine and cheese were being served outside and people were rising, talking, shuffling into the aisle.

Beth knew her time had come.

Mrs Brooke was giving her a quick hug. Gran was patting her on the shoulder and making encouraging noises. Tim was handing her the scores that she had left on her chair. "In case you need them," he said enigmatically. Then, in the voice of his old self, he added, "And good luck, Beth." She gave him a nod; it was all she could manage.

Megan met her in the vestry. The vicar and Mrs Hurst were there, thanking some of the performers. But after a while they were left alone.

"I can't do it," Beth blurted out.

Megan put her hands on Beth's arms and searched her face anxiously. "Beth, think. You know the sonata. You know what it means to Helen and to me. You will never forgive yourself if you don't play it now. Believe me, I have never forgiven myself, all my life. I can't let you repeat the same mistake." Beth gazed into Megan's intense grey eyes. Slowly, she nodded, "I have to do it, don't I?" she murmured.

She put down the scores. "Come on, then," she said with a new sense of purpose. "We haven't got much time, have we? Did you bring it?" But even as she spoke she saw the flat box. Megan lifted Helen's dress from the folds of tissue and helped Beth to put it on. Sash, pearls, her hair tied back with white ribbon: in a few minutes she looked and felt a different person.

Megan took a small mirror that was hanging on the wall and held it up for her to see the effect. The woman's eyes were very bright. "You look perfect," she declared. "Now, we have about five more minutes. Is there anything about the sonata you want to ask about?"

On the table next to the dress box was Helen's manuscript book. Beth picked it up and, in answer to Megan's question, she opened it at the page with the ink blot. "That's what scares me," she said with a shudder. "It always has."

"I know," Megan sighed.

"I've never been able to play the second movement right through. It makes me so ill. I get terrible pains in my chest. But I've told you that, haven't I?"

"I had those pains, too, remember, Beth. I know what it's like."

"Why does Helen do it? Why does she want me to feel what she felt when she died?"

Megan confirmed what she had already guessed. "I don't think she has any control over that. It has always prevented her from achieving her life's goal. I think, in some way, she wants to defeat her illness, too: she can only do that through the living. You mustn't think about it."

"What if I can't go through with it, Megan? Will she haunt me for ever, like she's haunted you?"

Megan shook her head, moved by the girl's distress. "If you find you can't play it all," she said, though her tone was doubtful, "then you'll just have to miss the most painful bit out. No one will really know, only you and I."

"And Helen. I don't think she would like that."

"No. But maybe she'll understand. Maybe she'll be here to help you."

Beth looked at Megan eagerly. "Do you think so? Here? Aren't spirits afraid of churches?"

That gave Megan pause for thought. "Evil ones are," she murmured, "and until now I've always regarded Helen as evil – after what she did to me - but now I see how trapped she was, how she had to find a way out. I don't know whether she'll be here; but look, Beth, she's brought you this far. Further than any of us. She won't desert you now, it's what she's fought for all these years."

"But how will I know she's here?"

"If she's here," said Megan quietly, a sudden catch of emotion in her voice, "you will know."

They were so engrossed in this conversation that they failed to hear Gran and Tim come in. Tim was holding a glass of orange squash for Beth. When Beth turned to face them, Gran gasped at her appearance. "Goodness me. Whatever have you done? What's going on here? Why have you changed? What are you wearing?"

"It's Helen," Tim said. "She's trying to look like Helen."

"Who? You mean that – that ghost girl?" Gran shook her head in disbelief.

Megan stepped forward. "Mrs Brooke," she began, "let me explain…"

But Gran wouldn't let her. The sight, the sound, of Megan, seemed to inflame her. "How dare you," she muttered. Her voice grew louder. "How dare you interfere with my granddaughter. I don't know what sort of hold you've got on her, what ideas you're putting into her head, but … but…" Gran spluttered to a halt. She was not able to put her finger on why the sight of her grand-daughter as Helen so disturbed her. "Beth," she demanded, turning to the white-faced girl. "Take that dress off. It's morbid. You've still got time. Take it off."

They all looked at Beth. Slowly, the girl shook her head.

"Beth," Gran repeated. "Take it off."

Beth looked at Gran unsteadily. "It's too late," she said in distress. "This is what I'm going to wear."

"You're upsetting her," Megan butted in. "She's about to play in a minute."

"Yes, that's all you care about," Gran spluttered. "I should have put a stop to you right at the beginning. She's not been herself since ... since..."

"Oh, Gran," Beth protested. "I'm doing all this because I *want* to, not because of Megan. Please don't try and stop me now." There was a short, tense silence. Tim broke it by handing Beth the orange squash. Beth took it as a peace offering.

Megan repeated, alarmed, "Please don't upset her, Mrs Brooke. She's..."

Gran did not let her finish. Throwing up her hands in despair, she turned and walked back into the church.

Tim grinned at his sister. "You look just like her," he said admiringly.

Beth put down her drink and, impulsively, she hugged her brother. Embarrassed, Tim backed away, but he smiled again and said, "I think what you're doing is very brave, Beth. I'll be with you all the way." Tears suddenly pricked his eyes. Without another word, he made his way back to his seat in the church, amazed at his sudden emotion.

The church was now almost full again. Dusk had fallen outside and candles had been lit on metal candelabras all down the sides of the church and around the altar and choir stalls. "Come and look, Megan," Beth whispered. "It looks beautiful."

Mrs Hurst and the vicar appeared again. Megan said to them, "Beth is all ready. But she has a surprise for the audience tonight. She has decided not to play what is on the programme." The vicar's eyebrows rose at this and Mrs Hurst looked at Beth enquiringly. "Instead," Megan continued, "Beth is going to play a sonata which was composed by a young ancestor of mine, Helen Murdoch. It's never been played in public before, and it's a wonderful piece. Beth identifies with it very closely. I'm sure you'll have no objection."

"Well, if that's what you want," Mrs Hurst murmured uncertainly.

"If you're quite sure," the vicar added, equally doubtful. "I'm sure you know best."

182

Beth said, "I'm going to say a few words about it first," she told him. "So you needn't say anything about it yourself."

The church was now in expectant silence. The vicar stood by the piano, which in the interval had been moved to the centre. Proudly, he announced Beth.

This is it, thought Beth. Keep a hold on yourself. You know what you're doing is right. She walked confidently from the vestry, past the choir stalls, through the rood-screen to the piano which gleamed in the spotlight. The applause was enthusiastic. When it had died down, there was a moment of such silence Beth did not know if she had the courage to break it.

"Tell them," Megan whispered behind her.

She clutched the edge of the piano. "I hope you don't mind," she began. She raised her voice. "I have decided to change the programme for tonight. Many of you have already heard me play the pieces in the programme at the concert I did a few weeks ago at school, so I hope you won't be too disappointed." She took a deep breath; so far,

183

so good. But, goodness, how difficult it was to say what you wanted to say, to get the words just right. "I am going to play a sonata tonight which none of you will have heard before. It was written by a girl of my own age called Helen Murdoch…" Beth felt her confidence growing. "Helen used to live in this village just before the first world war. Miss Murdoch here, who has been my teacher this summer, found Helen's sonata in the attic. We weren't sure until the last minute whether I would be ready to play it – it's quite difficult, you see, in parts – but I think I am now. I hope you will enjoy it." She sat down. Her heart was beating very fast.

There was a low murmur throughout the church. Beth glanced quickly at her family. Gran was whispering earnestly with her mother, but Tim was looking at her; he gave her a discreet thumbs-up sign.

Megan had opened Helen's manuscript book. Beth stared at it. The neat notation, with all its associations, gave her a strange feeling. Her heart continued to beat fast.

The church grew quieter.

She was in the act of raising her hands to the keyboard when her eyes were drawn to the shadowy corner of the church where the little plaque commemorating Helen's death was fixed. In the dark old chair beneath it a figure seemed to be forming. No one was sitting in the chair but Beth saw there was someone there. She strained her eyes to see.

Megan nudged her.

Beth brought her eyes back to the score. Here we go, she thought, and she began to play.

After the first few bars she barely looked at the music. She simply concentrated on the notes, how each should sound, the timing; nothing else mattered. The audience listened intently, curious: the music was a bit loud, a touch jagged in parts, but compelling. They began to forget that a child was playing it, that a child had written it; the music held them.

The first movement came to an end. She felt relieved that it had gone so well. Megan gave her a warm smile. Beth ignored the coughs and whispers of the audience. She was aware of feeling cold; there were goose pimples on her arms and her scalp was tingling. Her eyes were drawn back to the chair. She stiffened, drew in a sharp breath. No doubt about it this time – there was a figure in the chair. It was Helen.

The surface of the ghost seemed to waver slightly, like smoke from a candle flame. Beth could see the shape of the chair through the misty figure. Helen's dark, hollow eyes were fixed on her. Beth's coldness intensified. She shivered.

"What's the matter, Beth?" Megan whispered, alarmed at the way the girl was staring. Beth tore her gaze from the ghost. "She's here," Beth whispered. "She's sitting in that old chair. I can see her." Megan peered into the shadows; she could see nothing, but she did not doubt Beth's word. "She's here to help you get through the second movement," Megan said. "Do you want to play it? The audience are waiting."

The audience were becoming a little mystified. People began to murmur to one another.

Beth fixed her eyes on the score again. She began to think, I can't do it, I'll choke, I'll die…

Her glance was drawn back to the chair. It was empty. But relief lasted no more than a few seconds. Helen had risen from the chair and was floating towards her like a coil of mist. Beth felt a coldness all around her, like the dampness of a winter's night.

The ghost touched her. Curled around her. Merged with her. Was inside her.

Helen was lifting her hands. She began to play.

No one else knew what was going on, not even Megan. Beth was alone with the ghost. The church faded. There was only darkness now, a mist in her being, the sound of the sonata everywhere. But through it all, Beth was conscious of her heart beating in exact time with the music.

It began rather sombrely. Then it seemed to dance in a rather disordered way. Then the sombre theme reappeared, giving way to a long, lyrical piece. It was this which began to fragment, leading to the fateful moment in the score which marked Helen's death.

In that curious, misty limbo that Beth found herself in, she began to be aware of a pain in her chest, of a throbbing in her head, of breathlessness. But the strange thing was, it appeared to be happening to someone else, not to herself.

As the music progressed, the pain increased.

Then Beth became aware of Helen as a separate being within her. She felt Helen begin to shudder, to swirl like smoke in a bottle, to struggle as if she was seeking a way out. Beth played on, instinctively aware that the music was her lifeline: if she let that slip she would slide into the darkness.

Helen was now beginning to curl into one shape... They were approaching the fatal point in the music... The shape was like an oval ball now, tight and defensive... They were almost there... The ball was like a tiny baby in the womb... They had reached it... Beth felt a spasm of pain that made her falter...

And then she was through.

She played on, letting her hands and

memory do all the work, conscious only of a light stealing into the darkness.

She kept her eyes on the baby that was Helen and saw the child begin to grow, feeding on the music, growing in the light.

The second movement – the one that she had feared so much – ended in a sudden flourish.

She was damp with sweat. She tried to mop her brow and hands discreetly with a handkerchief that Megan slipped her. Megan said, "You did it, Beth, you did it; you got through. But you look exhausted. Are you sure you want to go on?"

The answer was in the girl's eyes: they shone with happiness. "She's inside me," Beth whispered. "And we came through it together…"

The audience were becoming restless again.

Beth glanced at them. They all seemed so unreal to her at this moment. She felt drained but full of light. She flexed her shoulder muscles and stretched out her hands, shaking off the tension of the last movement.

Then she launched into the third move-ment. She knew the worst was over. She particularly liked this movement, too. As she played, she was aware of Helen growing and stretching and maturing inside her, filling her being with a cold, misty light. When the movement reached its conclusion, they were once again indistinguishable, the only difference being Beth's heartbeat which continued to beat like a bass through it all. Distantly, she heard Megan say, "You're doing so well, Beth. I'm so proud of you." She turned a page of the score.

The final movement was Beth's favourite. It skipped about, full of impish energy; one minute it was a shooting star, the next the moon. Beth played with joy. She felt herself growing warm again. She was aware that Helen was fading inside her, just as mist is burnt off by the sun. Helen was reaching beyond her, she was rising out of her. She was leaving her…

For a moment the ghost of the girl was shimmering by the piano, smiling ecstatically at Beth. Her hair glowed; she looked reborn. Then she faded. As the music ended, so the last traces of Helen faded from the air.

"She's gone. She's free," Beth managed to whisper to Megan before the applause rose and deafened her. She stood and bowed. Somehow, the applause did not touch her. She was thinking of Helen floating away, dispersing among the stars.

After the concert, Beth and Megan had a moment to themselves in the vestry. Beth still felt intensely keyed up, her head full of space, stars, of Helen growing, breaking free, floating upwards. "Megan," she cried excitedly, clutching the woman's arms, "I've freed her. She was inside me, like a baby, and she grew and was herself again, and then she smiled at me. She's gone. We've freed her."

Megan hugged the girl. She felt tears film her eyes; if she had been on her own she would have sobbed out all the hurt the spirit had inflicted on her over the years, but now she could only postpone that. Beth was studying her face, sensing she was no longer a person to be afraid of. "You're free of her too," she whispered. "It's over, isn't it?"

"Oh, yes," Megan smiled weakly. "It's over

at last. Helen's got what she wanted. Now. Beth, you'd better get out of that dress."

But before she could do so, the vestry was invaded by her family, the vicar, Mrs Hurst and a number of others, including a photographer working for one of the local papers. He demanded pictures of Beth in Helen's costume and Beth had to pose for him. The photographer then took Megan aside to get the background details, leaving Beth to face her family.

"Well, young lady," said Gran with a slight edge of reproof, "you did give us a surprise. How long did you have that up your sleeve?" But at Beth's flush, her face changed to a laugh and she added, "You were wonderful, though. I can still hardly believe it."

"Well done," said Tim with fake heartiness, patting her on the back.

Beth's mother was uncharacteristically tongue-tied. On the way to the vestry she'd had to cope with a shower of congratulations from the audience, and now, looking at her daughter in that old-fashioned dress, she had the impression that she was looking at someone transformed, different, as if the music had broken a chrysalis and her daughter's wings were spreading. She felt a fine sense of self-recrimination too: how had she allowed herself to all but ignore Beth's talent, to treat it so lightly, as no more than a schoolgirl's accomplishment, when she was capable of this? She looked Beth in the eye and said, "I never realized how good you were until tonight. We must do something about it – I don't know what, but we'll do all we can from now, you'll see."

Beth was in too much of a whirl to take in what her mother was saying, but she nodded and suppressed a wish to laugh for sheer joy.

HIPPO GHOST

A Patchwork of Ghosts
Who is the evil-looking ghost tormenting Lizzie, and why does he want to hurt her...?
Angela Bull

The Railway Phantoms
Rachel has visions. She dreams of two children in strange, disintegrating clothes. And it seems as if they are trying to contact her...
Dennis Hamley

The Haunting of Gull Cottage
Unless Kezzie and James can find what really happened in Gull Cottage that terrible night many years ago, the haunting may never stop...
Tessa Krailing

The Hidden Tomb
Can Kate unlock the mystery of the curse on Middleton Hall, before it destroys the Mason family...?
Jenny Oldfield

The House at the End of Ferry Road
The house at the end of Ferry Road has just been built. So it can't be haunted, can it...?
Martin Oliver

Beware! This House is Haunted
Jessica is sure one of her stepbrothers wrote the note. But soon there are more notes ... strange midnight laughter ... floating objects... Perhaps the house really is haunted...

This House is Haunted Too!
It's starting all over again. First the note, and now strange things are happening to Jessica's family... The mischievous ghost is back – and worse than ever. Will they never be rid of it...?
Lance Salway

The Children Next Door
Laura longs to make friends with the children next door. When she finally plucks up courage, she meets Zilla – but she's an only child. So who are the other children she's seen playing in next door's garden...?
Jean Ure

And coming soon...

Ghostly Music
Richard Brown

Summer Visitors
Carol Barton

*If you like animals, then you'll love
Hippo Animal Stories!*

Thunderfoot
Deborah van der Beek
When Mel finds the enormous, neglected horse
Thunderfoot, she doesn't know it will change her
life for ever...

Vanilla Fudge
Deborah van der Beek
When Lizzie and Hannah fall in love with the same
dog, neither of them will give up without a fight...

A Foxcub Named Freedom
Brenda Jobling
An injured vixen nudges her young son away from her.
She can sense danger and cares nothing for herself –
only for her son's freedom...